WORD OF
Mouth

BY: EMANI SAWYER

Illustrated by:
Jewel Mason and Emani Sawyer

This book is dedicated to my late Great Grandmother.
She was the first person who showed me the power of words. Every time I saw her she told me:

"You are so beautiful, you can look at something ugly and make it pretty."
- Sarah Jane Stanford

Those words stuck with me and gave me confidence when I needed it. I hope these words do the same for you.

I would like to show my appreciation for all of my family that helped make this book possible. First, I would like to thank my Mom, Sabrina Sawyer, who has kept me encouraged through the hard times, when I thought I wouldn't finish. I would like to thank my best friend, my sister and book editor, Alia Wells, who I continuously bounced off ideas with and motivated me throughout the whole process. I would like to thank my brother, Jared Sawyer Jr., who assisted me with the publishing process. I would like to thank Jewel Mason for helping me illustrate my vision. Lastly, I would like to thank my dog, Nemo, and late dog, Jaliegh, who sat by my side as I wrote this book.

Thank You, Thank You, Thank You!!

Table of Contents

CHAPTER 1: The School Switcheroo 2

CHAPTER 2: Mean Girl 31

CHAPTER 3: Learning Curve 65

CHAPTER 4: Realization 153

ABOUT THE AUTHOR 270

As you read, feel free to illustrate thoughts here!

CHAPTER 1:

THE SCHOOL SWITCHEROO

It was 12pm, lunchtime at Harper Middle school. Diana had just sat down in the little blue chairs to eat her lunch. On the front of her lunch box it had a sticky note that read, "Have a great day my pretty girl! ~ From Mom," making Diana smile. Oh, how she loved her Mom's home-made lasagna. It made Diana's mouth water. She started eating as if she hadn't eaten breakfast that morning. Then, Jenna decides to sit right next to Diana. Jenna is the 6th-grade bully. She is notorious for giving everyone impolite nicknames and picking on them continuously without ever getting confronted. It was only the third day of school and Jenna had managed to already give almost everyone in her class a mean nickname and make them fear her presence.

"I guess it's finally my turn," Diana said in her head.

"Well, well, well, look who it is, Little Diana, who seems to not be getting fed at home. From the looks of it, you eat a little too much from where I'm sitting, Miss Pudge Pudge."

Diana looks away trying to ignore her comment.

"Awww did I hit a nerve? Is Miss pudge pudge upset? HaHaHa, pathetic."

"No, you're the one that's pathetic!"

"Oh, you dare talk to me like that? Why, what nerve you have Miss Pudge Pudge."

"Stop calling me that, Jenna," Diana said, trying to stay calm.

"I will call you whatever I feel like calling you, Miss. Pudge Pudge.

"SHUT your mouth Jenna and keep it closed!" Diana said a little too loud.

It became very quiet. Diana got everyone's attention with her outburst. The whole cafeteria was waiting for Jenna to say something, but she didn't. It was like she couldn't open her mouth. You could clearly see the veins sticking out of her neck as she tried desperately to speak. It was honestly a scary sight. All eyes were on Diana and she could feel them judging her. She didn't know what to do. She knew she was the cause of Jenna not being able to speak but had no idea how she did it or how to stop it. Then Jenna stormed out of the cafeteria and Diana thought it was over. So, she tried to continue eating her lasagna, but in her mind, she was trying to make sense of what had just happened. "Did she get locked-jaw? I heard that happens. Maybe she was just playing and she just wanted people to stare at her for attention. Yeah, yeah, that......makes no sense whatsoever," Diana thought to herself. But, she could still feel people staring at her. Then **Ding!** Saved by the bell. Literally. As she walked to class, she could hear people talking about what had just happened. She kept her head down and picked up her pace as she walked to her classroom. Once she sat down she heard "Diana Monroe, I need you to report to the principal's office," and her heart dropped to the floor and for the first few Moments, she couldn't move. She knew she was in huge trouble. Eventually, after her teacher, Mr. Gregory encouraged her to hurry along she walked to the principal's office. The pixelated window with the big black letters on the door made her freeze when she saw it, contemplating her fate. Once she walked inside she saw Jenna, still unable to speak with her veins still popping out her neck, pointing to Diana... blaming her for what was going on.

"What is the meaning of this Miss. Monroe? Jenna here, can't seem to speak and she wrote on a sheet of paper saying ``you are responsible," the principal, Mrs. Cally said.

"Well..."Diana said.

"Well, what Miss Monroe? Explain yourself this instant young lady," Mrs. Cally said in an assertive tone.

"I don't know how it happened ma'am...," Diana responded while searching for something to say.

"What do you mean you don't know? Obviously, you did something. Jenna cannot open her mouth. If you don't tell me what happened and how to fix it I'm going to call your mother."

"But mam, I really don't know how it happened".

"That is it, Ms. Monroe. I am calling your mother right now!"

The phone starts ringing...

"Hello?" Ms. Monroe said.

"Hello Ms. Monroe, I need you to come to the school. Your daughter has done something to another student causing her to not be able to open her mouth."

"That doesn't sound like my Diana…She's a good child," Ms. Monroe said.

"Well, your daughter claims she doesn't know what happened, but the student as well as the other kids in the cafeteria saw what went down. They said that they had gotten into a heated argument and Jenna's mouth wouldn't open; it has to be her doing. I just need you to come to the school, please, and try to persuade your child to tell us how to unglue or undo whatever she did to Jenna's mouth." Mrs. Cally said.

"Okay, I will be there shortly," Ms. Monroe said.

Minutes, more like hours, pass by while Mrs. Cally is trying to manually pry Jenna's mouth open and questioning Diana on how she did it. Then, Ms. Monroe finally arrives.

"What's going on Diana?" Ms. Monroe says as she runs over to Diana who happens to be crying in the office chair. "Why can't your friend talk?" she said.

"I… I… don't know Mommy," Diana says as she cries.

"Okay, okay, just tell me what happened from the beginning."

"I was at lunch and Jenna sat next to me and she started calling me Miss Pudge Pudge and I told her don't call me that and I told her to shut her mouth and then she just...stopped talking".

"Baby that's it?" Miss Monroe says confused. "Well that can't be it. Just telling someone to shut their mouth cannot actually cause them not to be able to open their mouth".

"It's not possible, she's obviously lying," the principal chimes in as she tooted her chin up.

"I'm not lying! I don't know what happened. Please, please just open your mouth already!" Diana yells.

"I'm trying! "Jenna blurts out, in shock that she was able to open her mouth again.

"I don't know how you just did that, but I consider you a danger to this school. I still don't know how you were able to get her to not be able to open her mouth in the first place, but I do know I cannot afford for this to happen to any other student on my watch. I will call security to escort you out."

"Get that freak away from me! Leave and never come back!" Jenna yelled.

"That's unnecessary, mam, we will just leave. Come on baby, let's go, we will talk about this when we get home, okay?" Ms. Monroe said calmly.

"Okay," Diana said, wiping her tears away.

The Monroe's pull up in their 2016 Honda Accord to their brick house on a hill. Diana is contemplating on what the talk will be about. "Will she be furious with me? How will she punish me? I didn't do anything...... I didn't do anything AT ALL. Ugh! I'm so confused." Diana thinks all of this while putting her head in her hands. She keeps replaying the whole situation in her mind and cannot find the answer. Ms. Monroe hasn't said anything the whole ride home. The silence was suffocating. Diana saw her home come into view as they pulled in the driveway. It's time. As they got out of the car and entered their home, Diana walked slowly, not knowing where this "talk" would happen, so she decided to take the initiative and sit at the living room table. Ms. Monroe hesitatingly sat across from her with a concerned, yet confused, look on her face.

"Okay baby… help me make sense of this. Wh- whh- what is going on?" Ms. Monroe caringly said.

"Mommy, I don't know, I don't know what is going on either. I didn't glue her mouth shut, I didn't tape it, I didn't touch her at all. I think she was faking it," Diana said.

"No Diana. I was there. She wasn't faking that," Ms. Monroe said in a serious tone.

"You're taking her side too. You think I'm a freak too?!," Diana said, getting upset.

"No, baby I don't think you're a frea-"

"She's a bully. She deserved it, she deserved to be scared, to feel like how she made everybody else feel around her!" Diana said, cutting her off.

"So, you did that to her because she was mean to you? It's only been three days."

"Three days too many."

"You can't just go doing whatever you did because a person is mean to you. You should have just gone to the principal."

"But you saw how she acted when Jenna said it was me. Mrs. Cally believed her and immediately blamed me, and the thought of Jenna simply faking it to get me in trouble didn't even pop up in her mind. Everyone is against me Mom, even you...," Diana said disappointingly.

"No, I am not against you, there are no sides. I just want to understand how this happened," Ms. Monroe said.

"Mom I seriously don't know, it's like she just did whatever I said like a game of Simon Says. I didn't even touch her," Diana said.

"I believe you, baby, I do. But, this cannot happen again, okay. I pulled some strings and texted a friend from the district office before we left the school, because I had a feeling they would react this way. He was able to get you enrolled into Carol Middle School."

"You mean the same friend who gave you the flowers that you keep in your room?" Diana said with a raised eyebrow and smirk on her face.

"...Yes, *that* friend," Ms. Monroe said hesitantly. "Go upstairs and wait while I get dinner ready and you will be able to go to your new school tomorrow.

"Okay."

Ms. Monroe, still confused. "What is going on with her? How did she command another child? Should I call a doctor? You know, maybe that girl was faking it. Yeah, yeah that's the only thing that makes sense. That is the only possible way this could happen," Ms. Monroe said to herself.

The next morning, Diana got dressed for school with her new navy-blue blazer, plaid pants, and two braids with ribbons fashionably tied in bows around them. Then, she ate breakfast. Oatmeal. Grits. Bacon. The whole shebang. The bus arrived at 6:30 as usual and Diana walked out the door. While on the bus,

Diana watches as the trees become blurred. She saw a brightly colored butterfly flying next to her window and she just knew it was a sign of good luck. It lifted her little spirit and a smile came out of the shadows as she approached her new school. It was enormous. The whole building seemed as if it was made of glass on top of the breathtaking landscape; further ensuring Diana this was going to be a new start and she would do the best she could not to do what she did to Jenna to anyone else ever again... whatever she did. As she walked the elaborate halls to her homeroom, no one really greeted her, not that she expected it, but it was as if nobody noticed she arrived and she liked that. She was blending in. During her first class, she made a friend, Brian. Brian was an excessive talker and annoyed Diana a bit with his constant babbling on how much he knows about astronomy.

"Do you know how many stars are in the sky? Huh do ya do ya?" asked Brian.

"No, I do not Brian." Diana, a little fed up with his talking, said.

"Well, we don't actually know, it's really too many to count. Isn't that just sooo interesting Diana? Just imagine being in space trying to count the stars. That would probably take forever. You know I am hoping to become an astronaut?" Brian asked.

"Oh really?" Diana says while putting her head in her hands slightly.

"Well I do. I would like to be an astronaut at NASA and possibly a rocket engineer if the whole astronaut thing doesn't go as planned. Do you know how many planets there are? Do you have a favorite? Huh Diana huh?".

"No, Brian I don't know how many planets there are and I don't really have a favorite planet. Astronomy just doesn't interest me the same way it interests you and we are supposed to be talking about the environment on Earth not outside of Earth; we are in life science right now, "

"Oh, alrighty then," said Brian as he scoots closer.

"I like you, Diana, you're my best friend!" Brian says as he hugs Diana a little too tight.

"We just met today how...Can you get off me please?" Diana asks sternly.

"Why stop now? I like long hugs, you are my best friend, you will get used to it," Brian states.

"No, I won't, " Diana said, struggling to stay calm.

"I'm still not letting gooo! We are gonna be best friends forever!" Brian exclaims.

"Is my teacher not seeing this?" Diana says in her head. "Okay, you need to get off of me Brian, I mean it."

"Nevverrr!" Brian says playfully.

"Just stay away from me! I don't want to be your friend anymore!" Diana blurts out a bit too loud. A minute later it was as if Brian appeared out of the door and couldn't seem to get in. "Did I do that? What is going on...what is wrong with me?" Diana contemplates in her head.

The teacher finally looks up from her computer and sees Brian attempting to get into the classroom door.

"Brian Come here right now," said Mrs. Pratt.

"I can't, I'm trying to Mrs. Pratt, I really am."

"Stop playing games this instant or I am going to get principal Myers," she explained.

"Oh no please don't call the principal," Diana said in her head.

"Ma'am I am not joking, come pull me. I cannot get through," Brian said.

"Okay, but when I prove that this was all just an act then you are going to write me a paper on why acting out in class is wrong, you hear me?" Mrs. Pratt asked.

"Yes mam," Brian said.

Mrs. Pratt gets out of her quirky chair and starts walking toward Brian. By this time Diana is officially creating a pool of her own sweat. Mrs. Pratt reaches for Brian's arms and tries to pull him in the room, but his feet won't budge. So, she then tries harder and tries again with all the might she could muster and still, Brian's feet wouldn't budge. Mrs. Pratt, finally believing Brian, is completely shocked.

"How...how did this happen?" Mrs. Pratt asked Brian.

"Oh no he is going to say I did it and I'm going to end up switching schools again," Diana said in her head while nervously biting her fingernails.

"Diana is responsible! She did this to me. I don't know how, but I know she did. It's like I just appeared over here after she yelled at me, everyone heard it right?" Brian asked.

"Yeah, we heard it,"" I heard it," "I think she's weird," "That's the new girl, right?" had been heard all over the classroom and is now filling up Diana's head like a not-so-delicious gumbo pot starting to boil and overflow.

Diana sat there stunned for a Moment, unable to speak, realizing something really *is* wrong. "This is the second time people are doing what I had told them to do. When is this going to stop? I can't keep moving schools," Diana contemplates internally.

"Diana what is the meaning of this? What have you done? Is this why you were kicked out of your last school, playing pranks on your fellow students? I will see to it that you are removed from my classroom. Better yet, I'll see to it that you get removed from this school," Mrs. Pratt asserts.

"But...but...I," says Diana.

"But what Diana? Unless you can tell me what's going on here and convince me that this is not your fault I don't want to hear from you," Mrs. Pratt said.

"But I want him to come inside the classroom too...I didn't mean to," Diana said on the verge of tears.

"Well I'm trying to...Woah...Woah," Brian says as he stumbles into the classroom.

Ignoring the fact that Brian just plopped into the room," So, you admit it then, you are responsible for this. You will face the consequences for your actions, young lady," Mrs. Pratt said.

"Yeah, you will pay, you will rue the day you crossed me! "Brian yells.

"Yeah, freak," said the other classmates while simultaneously sticking their tongues out at Diana and mocking her sadness.

Later that day before school ended, the principal had been called and Diana had been summoned. Then yet again, kicked out of school and her Mom was there to pick her up and take her home.

When Diana gets home, her mother is quite upset and explains to her that "This cannot and better not happen again, I can't keep calling in favors from my friend, he can lose his job for this. This is serious. You are building a record and I didn't raise you this way. You are going to go to Pedita Middle School and this is not going to happen again. Do you understand me, Diana?" Ms. Monroe said sternly.

"Yes," Diana said with her head hanging low.

Diana mopingly walked to her room. Her room was filled with plants, fake of course because when she had real ones they always ended up dying. There were trees in every corner. Her room had a nature vibe; her walls were painted with illustrations of the jungle with glow in the dark butterflies. She had pictures of animals from all over the world outlining the ceiling which was filled with light-up stars. When she walked inside her room and shut the door, she wanted to scream with frustration. She didn't understand why this had to happen to her and why it's happening now, out of the blue. Diana plopped on her bed filled with pillows and stuffed animals while looking at the ceiling with her mind racing about the new school that awaits her. She knew she couldn't let this situation get her down even though tears started to fall down the side of her face. She focused on the bright stars on the ceiling because if she were to wallow in the darkness that wished to consume her then that would be all she sees. She wanted the last school she went to, to be her new start.

This wasn't how she expected middle school to go. She thought she would just be getting more rigorous work, going to sports games, and maybe having a bit more freedom, not being the school freak everywhere she went. "It feels like a movie and I know movies are fake. So, this shouldn't even be happening to me at all, it makes no sense!" Diana thought to herself. She barely slept that night. The thoughts consumed her head, encasing it in a world pool of anxiety, fear, and confusion. She latched onto her last pinch of hope and used that as her fuel to allow her mind to be at peace and finally fall asleep.

Beep Beep!!

Diana is awoken from her sleep and is a little annoyed because it felt like she just went to sleep like an hour ago. Her eyes were sunken in from the lack of sleep, confirming her theory. However, it still didn't stop her from getting out of the bed and getting ready, because she was still hoping the day would go by smoothly. Her Mom woke up really early to make sure she could do her hair in the twist Diana liked. Ms. Monroe was doing everything she could to make sure Diana knew that she was there for her and was rooting for her.

Her Mom sat in the chair as Diana sat down on the floor. Ms. Monroe noticed Diana still wasn't being her usual smiley self and she could tell something was off.

"Are you excited about your new school today?" Ms. Monroe asked as she started twisting Diana's hair.

"Somewhat," Diana said

"Why aren't you excited, sweetie?"

"I'm just worried I will do something weird again."

"What have I always told you? You just can't live your life in fear. Fear makes you anxious. It is always better to be calm in situations like these because then you know you are confronting it with a leveled head to make the best decisions possible."

"I know Mom, but this thing keeps happening and I don't want to disappoint you again."

"Hey...hey," Ms. Monroe said in a soothing voice while lifting up Diana's chin. "I believe in you, whatever this is, we will deal with it together, okay? You aren't alone in this. Your Momma always has your back, don't you forget it," Ms. Monroe said, earning a dimple filled smile from Diana.

After finishing her hair...

"Okay it's time for me to take you to school, do you have your lunch box?"

"Yes."

"Do you have your bookbag?"

"Yes, ma'am it's on my back," she said jokingly.

"Do you have my love?"

"Always".

"Where is it?"

"Right here," Diana says as she points to her heart.

"Okay, then it is time to get in the car," Ms. Monroe said, motioning Diana to hurry along.

It felt like a very short ride to get to the school even though the GPS said it was only twenty minutes away. Diana was frozen for a second, looking through the window at her new and hopefully last middle school she'd ever attend. Her Mom noticed this, tapped her on the shoulder, and gave her the biggest hug she possibly could and gave her a big juicy kiss on the forehead, earning some seriously embarrassing glances from Diana. As soon as Diana gets out of the car and makes her way into the entrance doors, her Mom takes off, but not before she waves goodbye to her.

"Okay, here we go Diana, you got this," Diana says to herself.

Walking in, she sees colorful art paintings on the wall of butterflies and nature. This made Diana feel at home. Not realizing it, Diana had only stepped two feet into the school and had stopped to take in the scenery. Then she hears knocking on the door and she turns around to see a girl who looks like she could be her age and she says "Hey, you're kind of standing right in front of the door and I don't want to hit you". Diana, feeling embarrassed, swiftly shifted to the side and let the girl in.

"Sorry about that, I'm new here," Diana explained.

"You are okay, I could show you around if you want, we still have fifteen minutes before class starts.

"That would be nice, thank you, uhhh…" Diana said.

"Oh, I'm Stephanie, but you can call me Steph if you want," Steph stated.

"Okay, Steph. What grade are you in?"

"I'm in the 6th grade. So, technically I'm new too, but I learn super-fast. So, I know where everything is," Steph said confidently.

"That's great, can you take me to Mr. Campbell's class? He's my homeroom teacher?" Diana asked excitingly.

"OMG we are in the same homeroom, you know what that means right?"

"Thaatt we have the same teacher?" Diana said.

"No silly, it means we are meant to be best friends," Steph said excitedly.

"Oh goodness…," Diana said to herself, not someone else who feels like we should be best friends. I guess I can try….

Continues the conversation…

"Sure, I guess that would be cool," Diana said.

"Awesome!" Steph said.

"Okay, good job Diana," Diana said to herself. "You're doing just fine. You've made a friend and she actually seems pretty chill, that's good. You found your homeroom, that's good. You haven't made anything do things, that's good. You just have to get through the first day and the rest will be a breeze...hopefully," Diana tried to convince herself. As she walked into the classroom, she felt a sense of relief when the theme of the room was nature, just like her room at home. It was filled with ferns on the windowsills, the desks had animal print name tags on them. The teacher's desk even had a fish tank built into it filled with the largest Oscars she had ever seen, and to top it off there was a stereo playing relaxing rainforest sounds. It was another sign that this was the right place for her, yet it made her more determined than ever to not mess it up...again.

"You like it huh?" Steph asked.

"Oh, yeah how did you know?" Diana asked.

"You were practically drooling. You stopped and stood in the middle of the door like you did when you entered the school, so it was a logical assumption. I told you I learn fast," Steph said.

"Oh, I guess you do...," Diana said uneasily.

Diana frantically searches to find her name tag on the desks and she finally spots it on the second row closest to the window and she is satisfied. Especially since Steph, her new best friend is close but not too close to be all up in her personal space like Brian. Ugh...she shuddered at the thought of him being all over her. Diana sits down in her assigned seat and looks out the window. She turns her head as she hears the door close and her teacher Mr. Campbell enters the room and Diana notices that all the other seats have been filled, while she has been gazing out of the window. Mr. Campbell was a short stocky man with big glasses but had a great sense of style, she knew he had enjoyed dressing to impress and she wondered if he was going to keep it up all school year. Then he spoke and his voice, dare she say, did not match his features at all. It was very deep yet soft.

"Hello, class! We have a new student, her name is Diana (motioning towards Diana), everyone say," Hello, Diana!" Mr. Campbell announced.

"Hello, Diana!" the class shouted.

"Hiii," Diana said shyly.

"Okay everyone, today we will be watching a Stingray Science YouTube video and then you will split into groups to discuss what you have learned and relay that to the class," Mr. Campbell instructed.

Mr. Campbell turned off the main lights, which caused the room to go dim just enough for everyone to clearly see the video on the Promethean board. Diana was looking forward to the video, but not the groups nor the presentation afterward. The video was very interesting, it discussed the different biomes and how the animals are suited for their particular biomes. The instructor was able to show some animals from particular biomes and give us fun facts about them, on camera, that Diana enjoyed tremendously. She wondered if the lady kept all those animals in her house. Once the video shut off Diana got nervous, because it was time to get in groups and do the presentation in front of the whole entire class.

"Okay class, it is time for you all to get into groups of umm... let's say three and discuss what you've learned. You have 20 minutes to organize your thoughts to be ready for your group's presentation.

Given that you all are now in middle school, I would hope I don't have to put you into groups myself and that you guys would be able to pick your own groups. Am I right, class?" Mr. Campbell asked.

A resounding "Yesssss" filled the classroom. Diana immediately turned around in her seat to see if Steph was thinking the same thing she was thinking and before she knew it Steph was already approaching her desk and was asking her if she wanted to be in a group together. Diana, of course, said yes and then all that was left to do was to find one last person to be in their group. Diana and Steph looked around to see if anyone seemed as if they were isolated from the other groups and they saw a guy all by himself near the corner of the classroom. He seemed nice just based on his looks. He had a plaid shirt, ironed Khaki pants, and clean Air Force One's. Diana didn't know what, in particular, about his appearance that made him seem nice but she considered it a gut feeling. It was the same feeling she felt when she had seen Steph with her brunette hair, yellow shirt, blue jeans, and crocs and she was right then. So, she walked over to him and asked, "Hey, would you like to be in Steph and I's group?". Then he replied "Sure that would be great, I'm Tyson." The three kids arranged their desks to a little clump and started conversing about the video.

"So, what I learned was that animals have certain adaptations that help them survive in their biome," Steph said.

"I think we should also give examples of some of the traits that are helping the animals survive," Diana added.

"That's great. I think we should also add how humans have certain adaptations that help us survive in our environments and list them."

Tyson said.

"Okay, we have organized our thoughts. Now, we each should write about our topics and figure out the order we will tell the class and a conclusion," Steph said confidently.

"Okay, sounds like a plan," Diana said.

"I admire your leadership Steph," Tyson said, which made Steph's cheeks turn strawberry red.

While Steph desperately tried to hide her face and Tyson pretending not to notice, Diana was trying to make sure she worded her part carefully. After about five minutes of them working independently, they joined together to discuss how they would end it. Tyson suggested that they could simply say "And with that being said, we enjoyed the video. Thank you," all together in unison and the girls agreed.

"Okay class, it is time for you all to present what you have learned to the class. Who would like to go up first?" he asked as he motioned towards the front of the classroom.

Steph immediately raised her hand and said "We will do it. We'll be the first to present!" Diana was flabbergasted because they definitely didn't agree on that. She felt the temperature of the room drop, as her nervousness skyrocketed. Tyson seemed to be okay with it. So, they went up to the front of the classroom as a group while the rest of the students peered back at them with their dull expressions. Steph started it off and she did well and the class was paying attention. Tyson was next with his points and he did pretty good as well, as the class got more and more into the presentation. Lastly, it was Diana's turn to take the stage. She started off a bit rough but as she kept going the more confident she grew, the louder her voice, and the more attentive the crowd got. Miraculously, they were able to say their last line in unison and the students, along with Mr. Campbell, clapped for them. They then looked at each other, smiled, and took their seats.

The next presentations also went great and Steph made sure to clap violently for everyone, which the other kids seemed to both enjoy and find annoying at the same time. Before Diana knew it, it was time to go home. "My first successful day of middle school completed," she thought.

As Diana walked out the classroom door, she waved to Steph and said

"Bye, I'll see you tomorrow."

"Bye, can't wait!" Steph exclaimed.

Tyson had already left the classroom before she could say goodbye, but she thought nothing of it. As Diana waited for her Mom's car to pull into the car-riders area, she decided to go ahead and look in her book bag to make sure that she hadn't forgotten anything and sure enough, she forgot her notebook that had her homework assignment in it. She proceeded to run back inside the building and finally reached her classroom and saw the lights pitch black and the door locked, but she needed to get inside.

"I know there's a janitor somewhere around here that has a key and could hopefully help me," Diana thought.

So, Diana ran around frantically trying to find a janitor, any janitor, to help her get in the classroom. Then after about five minutes of walking/jogging, she found him.

"Umm Mister Vendetta?" she read from his name tag.

"Yes, that is my name," replied Mr. Vendetta.

"I left my notebook with my homework in it in my classroom and it's locked, can you help me?" Diana pleaded.

"Sure, I can help you," Mr. Vendetta said with a kind smile.

"Who's your teacher?" he asked.

"Mr. Campbell," Diana replied.

"Okay, let's go. I assume you're in a hurry, you came from the car-rider area," Mr. Vendetta inferred.

"Yes, I am. I don't want to be late for my Mom," Diana replied.

Diana and her new friend, Mr. Vendetta, walked to the room and he found the key surprisingly fast. Diana was able to find her notebook stuck in the back of her desk compartment.

"I'm glad you found what you needed," Mr. Vendetta said.

"Me too, thank you for your help Mr. Vendetta," Diana said.

"You're quite welcome. What's your name?" Mr. Vendetta asked.

"My name is Diana!" Diana said as she ran out the double doors.

Diana came out right on time because within five minutes her Mom was there to pick her up. Diana knew her Mom had been worried because the first thing her Mom asked her when she got in the car was if *IT* happened again, to which Diana replied "No," and an immediate look of relief flashed on Ms. Monroe's face.

"What would you like to eat today? I'll let you decide since you had a successful first-day at your new middle school," Ms. Monroe asked Diana.

"Can we eat your famous spaghetti?!," Diana asked excitedly.

"Yes, anything for my baby" Ms. Monroe replied.

That night, Diana went to sleep hopeful that tomorrow was going to bring more sunshine.

CHAPTER 2:

MEAN GIRL

The next day went about the same as the first. Mr. Campbell structured the classroom with groups consisting of three desks, in which Diana, Steph, and Tyson sat in and did their assignments. Mr. Campbell said he liked to switch up the classroom sometimes to keep things interesting and Diana respected him for that, especially since she often bored easily. There was no presentation and everything was going well until lunch time.

The first day she went to lunch, she was able to chill with Steph and Tyson. The food was actually pretty good. No one bothered her like what she had experienced before at the other school. This day, sadly, was different.

Diana walked into the cafeteria filled with the noise of middle school gossip. Her friends sat at the same long black table they did yesterday. After they had talked for a while, Diana felt a girl brush against her back harshly and she turned around to see another girl looking back at her as if Diana was the one who had bumped into her when there was a large enough walkway for her to have walked past. This made Diana upset, especially because the girl didn't apologize, in fact, she laughed and walked along. Diana was just about to say something and then she remembered what happened last time and stopped herself. Steph and Tyson, having watched what went down, were also clearly upset, especially Steph. Her face turned bright red and then she proceeded to get out of her chair and walk towards the girl who had bumped Diana. Diana gets up to try and stop her, but Steph was quick on her feet and had gotten to the girl before Diana got there.

"That wasn't nice," said Steph in a harsh tone.

"What wasn't nice?" the girl said.

"You bumped into her on purpose and didn't apologize. So, you need to apologize," Steph insisted.

"No, what you need to do is get out of my face!" the girl exclaimed as she started to get up.

"No, you're the one who needs to…."

"Steph, stop!" Diana said, desperately not wanting this to escalate.

Immediately Steph's mouth shuts closed.

"Thank you for taking up for me, but if she wants to be mean then let her. She doesn't faze me. Let's go back and eat the rest of our food before it's too cold," Diana said as they started walking back to their table.

Meanwhile, Tyson was sitting there with a concerned look on his face.

"What happened over there?" Tyson asked.

"Don't worry about it." Diana said while Steph sat there silently.

"You know, I heard about her from the 7th graders. They say she's the classic mean girl…like in the movies."

"Dang another one….," Diana said a little too loud.

"Huh?" Tyson asked.

"Nothing, but okay I know to look out for her now then. Thanks," Diana said

"No problem," Tyson said.

Steph still hasn't said a word and Diana was starting to get worried. Did she do it again? Steph didn't look uncomfortable or like she was trying to speak but couldn't. However, Diana couldn't ignore it, but how could she ask without exposing her secret or looking suspicious. She had to choose her words carefully.

"Hey, Steph... are you okay?" Diana asked, hoping Steph would say *something*.

Steph looked like she was about to speak, but motioned that her throat was hurting or sore. Diana couldn't tell though and kept eating.

"Oh, your throat hurts. Well I hope you feel better soon," Diana said nervously, she even started to sweat a bit.

"Please speak again," Diana said desperately, earning a confused look from Tyson but surprisingly not from Steph.

Steph still hadn't said a word when they reached the classroom door and Diana started to twirl her hair around her fingers out of nervousness. Mr. Campbell liked active participation in the classroom and started asking the class questions but Diana couldn't pay attention. She was too scared that she did something to Steph.

Luckily, Mr. Campbell didn't call on Diana and the class ended as usual, but Steph still hadn't said a word, even Tyson was picking up on it.

All Diana did was worry when Steph practically ran out of the classroom after the bell rang and she couldn't catch up to her. Diana hoped she was okay and that her throat really wasn't hurting, but something inside told her that that wasn't the case.

Diana didn't tell her Mom about what happened and tried to keep calm on the way home. It was hard to do since her heart was beating out of her chest. Ms. Monroe could tell that Diana was acting, but trusted her enough that if Diana needed to tell her something then she would tell her. She had always told Diana she could come to her about anything. After dinner, Diana quickly went up to her room and changed into her pajamas. She laid in her bed hoping Steph was feeling better and that she started talking once she got home. However, she knew it would not help if she worried all night and got no sleep. So, she tried her best to fall asleep and after about twenty minutes of her staring at the stars on her ceiling, sleep took her under.

Steph

"Ooh I wonder what's for lunch today," Steph thought in her head as she walked with Tyson and Diana to the Cafeteria. Steph was relieved when she saw the table they sat at yesterday was available. They were eating for a while, talking, laughing, and then this girl just ran into Diana on purpose and did not apologize. "How dare she! And Diana is going to sit there and take it? No no, not my best friend," Steph thought to herself. So, Steph gets up and sprints to the girl who bumped into Diana, taps on her shoulder, and says…

"That wasn't nice," in a harsh tone.

"What wasn't nice?" the mean girl said.

You bumped into her on purpose and didn't apologize. So, you need to apologize," Steph insisted.

"No, what you need to do is get out of my face!" the girl exclaimed as she started to get up.

"No, you're the one who needs to…."

"Steph Stop!" Diana said, desperately not wanting this to escalate.

Steph was about to continue anyway but when she tried she couldn't. She couldn't even open her mouth. She tried to keep a straight face, but on the inside, she was freaking out. "What is this? What's happening to me? How did it happen? Did Diana…no no that can't be it. It literally does not make sense," Steph thought in her head. Before Steph knew it, she and Diana were walking back to the table. Steph could not focus on eating and she certainly couldn't talk. So, she decided to try and figure out how this happened. She replayed the whole scenario in her head step by step...word by word. She heard "Stop Steph" right before she couldn't open her mouth. "Could that have been it?" she thought. "But that doesn't make any sense..." Steph frustratingly contemplated. Then she heard Diana say...

"Hey, Steph...are you okay?"

Steph didn't want to cause suspicion. So, she thought on her feet and decided to tap her throat, making it seem like her throat was hurting and she couldn't speak. She wouldn't really be lying because she, in fact, couldn't speak. Luckily, it seemed enough for Diana and Tyson to drop it. Diana probably asked that because Steph was being unusually quiet and drifting off in space. So, Steph started to pay more attention to the conversation from that point forward to make sure she didn't come off as *too* weird.

"Oh, your throat hurts. Well I hope you feel better soon," Diana responded

"Please speak again," Diana said under her breath.

"Wait what?" Steph thought. "Why would she say that? Does she know I really can't talk? How could she know-" Steph contemplated. "You know what, maybe that's why she is coming to the school later in the year, maybe she was kicked out because something like this happened before. I haven't known her for long, but I have a feeling that she isn't usually the kind of person who would just let something like that happen to her and do nothing about it. I know it's just a hunch but, does she have some kind of power? Grandma Lulu used to talk to me about something like voodoo or something where spirits and ghosts are real so maybe powers can be real too and I think Diana confirmed it by asking me that. Okay, so I figured out she has some kind of power but that doesn't change the fact that I still can't speak. I can't ask her in front of Tyson. I'm quite sure Diana doesn't want anyone to know. Maybe it will wear off...yeah...hopefully..." Steph thought to herself. Her mind was racing with thoughts about magic and most importantly, Diana and how she fits into all of it.

When lunch was over Steph, Diana, and Tyson all walked back to class.

In class, it was taking Steph all she could to not raise her hand to answer questions, but she had to keep up the facade for Diana's sake. So, she kept quiet throughout the whole class. She couldn't risk lollygagging after class with Diana and Tyson because she knew she wasn't the best actor. So, she made a plan. She would bolt out the classroom as soon as the bell rang, and hopefully, Diana and Tyson would think she really had to use the restroom or something…" yeah…that could work" Steph thought. So, when the bell rang she stuck to her plan and ran out of the classroom to the car-riders' pickup and crossed her fingers hoping her Dad was there to pick her up on time. Thankfully, he was.

"But what am I going to say to him? Ughh, too late I'm almost at the car, improv it is," Steph thought. Steph opens the car door, hops inside the car, and buckles her seatbelt all in one fast and swift motion. "Hmm, maybe I could have a power too. Speedy Steph could be-," Steph thought as her Dad interrupted.

"Hey, how was school today Steph?" Mr. Ansberry asked.

"Oh no what do I do? …umm I got it," Steph thought.

Steph then decided to give him the widest smile she could, not being able to actually open her mouth and gave him a thumbs-up, hoping he would buy it.

"That's great sweetie" Mr. Ansberry

"Yes, I did it," Steph said in her head.

Their car ride was pretty long, but her Dad, luckily, liked to jam out to music in the car instead of talking. Steph tried to distract herself by looking at the scenery outside the window, but it wouldn't work. During the entire car ride, Steph was worried that her voice would either not come back at all, that Diana had to reverse it, or that it would stop working after a while. When they finally arrived at their home and walked inside, Steph felt this feeling of relief all through her body and wondered if that meant Diana's spell or powers had worn off and she could speak again. She walked in to see her Mom cooking dinner and ran to her and gave her a big hug and said...

"Hey Mom, I missed you," Steph said, thankful it actually came out her mouth.

"Hey Steph, I missed you too hun. Are you almost ready for dinner?" Mrs. Ansberry asked.

" You know it," Steph replied.

Later that night, after Steph's parents kissed her goodnight, she thought to herself how cool it is going to be to have a best friend with superpowers. She then decided she needed to get some sleep and slowly drifted off to sleep excited for tomorrow.

Diana

Tomorrow came and Diana was getting ready for school, hoping to see her best friend smiling and talking when she got there. Her Mom made her some pancakes and eggs for breakfast which she thoroughly enjoyed and then they were off to school. When Diana arrives at school, she searches for Steph since they usually arrived around the same time. She didn't see her right off the bat so she decided she would wait for her at the classroom door. She had ten minutes until class was supposed to start. It wasn't until eight minutes after that that Steph came and Diana didn't see her sneak up behind her.

"Hey, Diana," Steph said with a huge smile on her face.

"Hey, Steph I'm happy your throat is doing better today. What do you think it was...?" Diana curiously asked.

"Oh, nothing just...Your powers," Steph said with a smirk.

"Yep, my.... what? ..... I- I... don't have powers. What are you talking about, is your head by chance messed up too? What did you eat yesterday?" Diana asked, trying to convince Steph it wasn't her.

"Nice try, but I've already figured you out, Diana. You got kicked out of your other school for an incident like yesterday and you don't want anyone to know about your powers." Steph said confidently. She felt like a detective...maybe solving mysteries could be her power.

"But...How did you figure it out?" Diana asked.

"You literally just told me out of your mouth. I knew it! I mean...I did know it, but it was also a long shot. But, you just confirmed it. That is so cool."

"I can't believe I just told on myself," Diana said to herself while running her hands down her face dramatically.

"My best friend has superpowers. My best friend has superpowers," Steph paraded around a bit too loud.

"You can't say that too loud. You really can't. If people find out, I might get kicked out again. I'm begging you please don't tell anyone. If you really consider yourself to be my best friend you would keep this secret for me," Diana insisted.

"Couldn't you just force me to keep the secret like how you forced me not to talk yesterday?" Steph asked.

"Umm, I don't know, but I don't think it would be right if I did that. To be honest I don't even know how it *really* works. Or if it's actually powers or not," Diana said. She realized that she had been worrying so much about hiding her powers that she didn't even understand exactly what they were or how they worked.

"Oh, you definitely have powers, Diana. What happened yesterday was not some kind of coincidence or fluke. I felt the effects wear off when I got home." Steph said

"Okay, well at least I know it wears off eventually. Or it's a distance thing. I don't know. There are too many unknowns."

"Well, that's why I'm here. Your own personal practice dummy," Steph said.

"I don't think that is a good idea Steph. What if I were to hurt you?" Diana asked.

"I don't care," Steph said.

"Well, you should care. And I would actually care if you got hurt by me," Diana said.

"I know you wouldn't hurt me. We are best friends. And plus, you're just a nice person in general," Steph said.

"One, we haven't known each other for that long, even though I do consider myself a nice person. Two, of course, I wouldn't WANT to hurt you, but it is a real possibility that I could and I don't want to risk it. Plus, what if others were to see me practicing on you? I would get made and be kicked out," Diana said while leaving out the fact she couldn't afford to switch schools again.

"One, I'm very aware we haven't known each other for that long, but I get good vibes from you and my gut is never wrong and you just confirmed that you are a nice person. Two, you really do want to try it out because you wouldn't have considered the possibility that others would see us if you truly didn't want to try it all," Steph said confidently.

"Oh, you're good..." Diana said, realizing Steph read her like a book. Steph was very persistent and uniquely persuasive.

"Oh, I know," Steph said smiling because she knew she was winning this debate. "And as far as people finding out, I know a place where we can go after school where no one would see us," Steph insisted.

"Are you sure...like are you really sure?" Diana asked.

"Yes, yes trust me on this Diana. I wouldn't steer you wrong," Steph said.

"Okay." Diana agreed.

"I really hope she doesn't," Diana said to herself as they walked into the classroom. Mr. Campbell gave them a pop quiz that day on biomes and luckily Diana liked that video he showed them the day of the presentations so much that she watched it over and over or she would have failed. Steph had a grin on her face so Diana figured she felt confident as usual and Tyson didn't have a grin, but he wasn't frowning either so Diana took that as he was doing okay on the quiz.

As it started nearing the end of class, Diana couldn't stop thinking of her and Steph's practice coming up. "Would we do it today after school? Or tomorrow How long is it going to be? Where would it be?" Diana contemplated with herself. "Well, it can't be today because my Mom wouldn't know to pick me up later after school," Diana decided.

It was the end of class and Diana walked to Steph's desk as fast as she could and Steph said….

"Okay, so do you wanna do this tomorrow? Or when can we do it? I'm pretty much free any day," Steph asked. She was buzzing with excitement and it was rubbing off on Diana.

"Tomorrow is okay. What should I tell my Mom?" Diana asked.

"Umm you should say that you joined a club," Steph suggested.

"Okay…okay, I'll say that I joined an art club. She likes my drawings so she should believe it, hopefully," Diana decided.

"Okay, sounds like a plan. Team...Teammmm...we have to come up with something. All the greats have a name," Steph said with a chuckle.

"Yeah we do," Diana agreed.

"See you tomorrow, Diana!" Steph exclaimed while waving goodbye.

"Bye, see ya," Diana said, waving back.

When Diana got in the car, she and Ms. Monroe exchanged their usual greeting-Hay, how was your day? Good, how was yours? Good. That's good - the usual. Then Diana asked...

"Guess what Mom?"

"What baby?" Ms. Monroe replied.

"I decided to join an after-school art club," Diana replied back.

"That sounds great, baby girl," Ms. Monroe says.

"The meetings start tomorrow after school," Diana stated.

"Okay, what time do they end?" Ms. Monroe asked

"Umm I didn't ask.... he...hehe..sorry," Diana said.

"It's alright I'll be outside waiting at 4:30. I don't want my baby sitting outside waiting on me," Ms. Monroe said while kissing Diana on the forehead.

"Okay," Diana replied with a bright smile on her face. Ms. Monroe was glad she was settling in at the new school. Things were really starting to look up for Diana and she couldn't be happier for her baby girl.

After Diana had eaten her dinner, it was time to go to bed and all Diana could think about was her "art meeting" tomorrow. She tried to focus on the waterfall sounds playing through her CD player. It was supposed to help her fall asleep, but even those weren't working. The waterfall sound only made Diana want to pee. After listening to them for about an hour, Diana got up, walked to her counter, and cut it off, leaving her with complete silence.

Usually, Diana loved sweet silence. But that night it only made the thoughts in her head scream louder, the thought of possibly hurting Steph and the opposite, being really happy she figured out what her power was and how it really works; it was a constant battle. However, she knew she shouldn't dwell on it for long so after a while she started to meditate to get her thoughts to quiet and relax so she could be in the right headspace to be able to sleep. Luckily, it worked and she was able to fall asleep. The tug of war in her mind was put on pause to deal with on another day.

The next day, Diana woke up refreshed and ready to go to school. She was still a bit nervous about practicing with Steph, but still ready to at least give it a try. "After all, it would be great to get in control of this thing," Diana thought. That morning went by swiftly since her Mom was running late for work and Diana had to rush to get ready so she could get dropped off at school. In the car, Diana made sure to mention to her Mom about the "art meeting" after school so she would remember to pick her up late.

When Diana got to school, she saw bright-eyed Steph and immediately felt anxious and excited.

"Hey, Diana!" Steph said practically running towards Diana to hug her.

"Hey, Steph!" Diana said as they embraced each other.

"Are you ready for practice today…huhhhh?" Steph said excitedly, nudging up against Diana's shoulder.

"Yes, I am still very nervous but excited," Diana said.

"Let's go ahead and get to class," Steph insisted.

"Alright," Diana said while walking towards their classroom.

Throughout the whole class, Diana and Steph were sharing glances and chuckles. Tyson was picking up on it and wondered what was going on.

It was lunchtime and Tyson wanted to see if he could pry it out of them.

"So, do you two want to let me in on whatever y'all keep laughing about?"

"Oh...we were laughing...umm it was because of a joke we heard about," Diana said. Meanwhile, Steph is experiencing second-hand embarrassment due to how terrible Diana's lying skills are.

"Oh really, so what was this joke? I want to hear it," Tyson asked while putting his hand under his chin and squinting his eyes.

"Oh....umm the cow that's old...umm its milk comes out powdery haha. Wait the milk doesn't come out at all the powder does...haha..ha" Diana said with the biggest, fakest smile she could.

Tyson, clearly not believing it said, "Okay...I guess that's funny" as he leans back in his chair.

"You know what...The joke was so terrible we thought it was funny," Steph chimed in.

"Oh yep, that's what happened," Diana said.

"Oh okay, I get it now," Tyson said, nodding his head.

Tyson wasn't that gullible, but he knew he wasn't going to be able to get it out of them. So, he decided he would keep a low profile and find out what was going on, on his own. Tyson was a walker and his parents didn't get off work until 9 o'clock. So, he would be able to stay after school and see what they were up to. "There is no way they were laughing at that *lame* joke Diana made up. They have to be up to something to be acting so weird," he thought.

Lunch was over so everyone went back to the classroom. Diana was sure with Steph's help they covered their tracks with Tyson. Steph wasn't as sure, but she was hopeful. When they got back to the classroom, Diana and Steph didn't laugh as much to try and make it seem like everything was normal. Tyson was coming up with a plan on how to follow the girls without them catching him. He decided he would use the detective skills he got from watching cop shows to use and make sure to stay where they couldn't see him and move when they moved.

When the bell rang for class to be dismissed, the girls got together outside the classroom door to discuss a few things.

"Hey, so where are we going to practice?" Diana asked.

"There's this abandoned courtyard in the old part of the school no one uses anymore," Steph said.

"That sounds a bit suspicious, but I'm desperate so okay I'll go," Diana said.

"Okay let's go," Steph said.

"Wait. Do you think Tyson is on to us?" Diana asked.

"Umm…he might be, but I highly doubt he would follow us just because we, or should I say you, are a terrible liar," Steph said.

"Well, I'll have you know that most people view that as a good thing," Diana insisted with her head held high.

"Yes, when the lie doesn't depend on them getting caught," Steph said.

"Touché," Diana said.

"Alright, but seriously let's go. Tyson is getting up. It's better to be safe than sorry. It's this way," Steph said hurriedly while pulling Diana down the hallway.

The girls made many twists and turns. Some were needed but others were just to throw Tyson or anyone off in case they were following them. Little did they know that Tyson saw through their tactic and ended up guessing where they were headed based on the first few turns. Tyson went to the summer program and on the tour, they showed him, as well as the other kids, where the older sector of the school was. He knew that all the old classroom doors were locked so the only place they could go was this long, weird hallway or the courtyard. So, instead of directly following the girls, he followed his gut and went straight to the abandoned sector of the school and found a place to hide in the corner behind a trash can. He sat there for a good five minutes and almost gave up hope, but then the girls arrived laughing. Luckily, he hadn't been spotted and watched the girls go into the courtyard. When he knew they wouldn't see him, he walked towards the double doors that led to the courtyard and peeked through the crack in the door hinge, at that vantage point he could hear and see everything if he stayed quiet. "If they did all this just to do some stupid flips I'm going to be upset," Tyson thought to himself.

"Okay Diana, time to get a grip on that power of yours," said Steph

"I'm ready," Diana said.

*"Diana has powers? No way..." Tyson said to himself while covering
his mouth.*

"Okay, I guess you just have to tell me to do something. So, tell me to do something."

"Okayyy...Umm...start dancing," Diana instructed.

They waited a few seconds and..., "Didn't work," Steph said.

"I really don't know how it works," Diana said.

"Okay, maybe you have to say it with more authority," Steph suggested.

"Okay, I'll try that. Start dancing!" Diana yelled....and nothing happened

"Maybe you have to stand in a power pose. Have you heard of it before?" Steph asked

"No, I haven't. What is it?" Diana asked.

"You stand really wide, feet spread apart, tilt your head up, and put your hands on your hips with your hands in a fist," Steph explained.

"Okay," Diana said while getting in position.

"So, do you feel more confident?" Steph asked.

" Yes, actually. That's really cool. Who taught you that?" Diana asked.

"My Grandmother did, but go ahead and try again now?" Steph insisted.

"Okay. Steph, I command you to start dancing!" Diana yelled and yet again, nothing happened.

"We just have to keep trying, let me think for a Moment," Steph said.

"No Steph. Let's just stop. I probably don't have any powers. It was just a weird coincidence or something," Diana said with her head down.

"No, I know what I felt. It wasn't a coincidence. I just have to think."

"Umm...what has been a constant in the situations where it happened before?" Steph said.

"Um...Usually, someone makes me upset," Diana explained.

"Okay, maybe that's it. You just have to get mad," Steph said excitedly.

"Okay..." Diana said.

"...Sooooo go ahead get angry!" Steph encouraged.

"I can't get mad for no reason Steph and I really don't like to get angry," Diana explained.

"Well, do you want to figure this thing out or not?" Steph asked.

"I do, I really do," said Diana.

"Okay then let's make you upset," Steph said.

"I'm ready," Diana said.

Steph was now in analysis mode. "What could make Diana mad?" she thought to herself. "Come on Steph, you got this. What have you noticed about Diana? Well, she doesn't usually sit close to anyone except me or give hugs to me and maybe Tyson every now and then. So, she might like her personal space. Maybe I can get all in her personal space and annoy her? Or...she wouldn't mind cause I'm me. So, I should think of something else. Umm...I've never seen her with her Dad before? Maybe there is something there. She also wears baggy shirts which is a sign she either likes baggy clothes or wants to hide her stomach. Okay, I think I.... I think I have a game plan now." Steph says to herself.

"How come I don't see your Dad around?" Steph asked.

"I don't really want to talk about him," Diana said

"Did he not care about you and your Mom enough to stay?" Steph asked.

"I don't know. I'd like to think he cares about us, but I really don't want to talk about him Steph."

I don't care what you want to talk about. You're sad he left you huh?" Steph asked.

"I told you I don't wanna talk about it, Steph!" Diana said as tears welled in her eyes.

"Why is Steph being so mean? That's so unlike her to do that to Diana,"
Tyson thought to himself.

"Steph, stop it. I know you are trying to help by acting this way but you're really making me upset." Diana said as a tear streamed down her cheeks.

"Oh, am I? I'm just getting started...Aww, are you crying? Boohoo my Daddy left me and whenever I think about it I cry and eat a muffin," Steph said.

"I- I don't do that," Diana said.

"Well it sure looks like you do, you should consider losing a couple of pounds."

"And you should just...just get away from me Stephanie!" Diana screamed.

Immediately Steph's legs started to walk backward from Diana.

Diana is trying to calm down and wipe her tears, not noticing Steph uncontrollably walking away.

"Umm Diana, it worked," Steph said uneasily.

"What worked? You made me upset. Congrats, you got what you wanted. I don't want to talk to you!" Diana yelled as she turned her back to Steph.

"No, your powers...I- I can't stop myself," Steph said.

"Well, great cause I don't wanna see you right now anyway," Diana said, looking back and noticed Steph walking away.

"But...Diana, I need you to stop it," Steph begged.

"Why would I stop it?"

"Because if you don't then I'm going to eventually get hurt," Steph explained.

"How can you get hurt? It's a courtyard, there's nothing here".

"Yes, yes there is. There's a road at the bottom of the hill at the edge of the courtyard."

"What...? Well, how do I stop it?" Diana asked urgently, realizing the depths of the situation.

"I don't know! I just know I'm starting to see the road and I don't wanna die," Steph said with a tremble in her voice.

"You don't have any ideas?! See, this is why I didn't want to do this," Diana said while thinking of what she was going to do, with her hands on her head.

"Well it's too late now, help me," Steph pleaded.

"Oh, No Steph is in trouble! I have to help her, but how?" Tyson thought to himself. Then he felt a tap on his shoulder and his heart sank.

"What are you doing here?" Mr. Vendetta asked.

"Oh umm...nothing looking at the scenery...Hehe" Tyson said.

"I'm old, not stupid. What is Diana and her friend doing? If they keep going, they are going to run into a road down that hill...I need you to tell me what happened...Everything" Mr. Vendetta insisted.

Tyson hesitated. Steph needed help, but Diana had a secret to keep. "Okay...this is going to sound crazy but I promise I'm not lying...Diana has this superpower where I'm guessing it only works when she is angry. Then Steph got her angry and Diana said "get away from me" and now Steph can't stop moving backward away from Diana and Diana doesn't know how to stop it and-." Tyson quickly said in one breath.

"Oh no... I need to go." Mr. Vendetta said.

"Okay, what should I do?" Tyson said.

You should probably go home, son." Mr. Vendetta said.

"But, I wanna help, I can-".

"I said Go home!" Mr. Vendetta yelled.

Then immediately Tyson's legs started walking in the direction of his house...What is this...What's happening to me... He has...No way...he's like Diana!

"Okay, I'll try and pull you back?"

"I don't think that's going to work. The closer you get to me, the faster I go," Steph said.

"Oh my gosh...What do I do?" Diana said, trying to keep up with Steph.

Then she heard footsteps behind her. It was Mr. Vendetta. They were going to be in so much trouble now. "Could this get any worse?" Diana thought.

"Diana!" Mr. Vendetta exclaimed.

"Oh, thank goodness. Grab Steph she's going to keep walking till she runs into the traffic," Diana couldn't worry much about being caught when Steph was in danger.

"It won't work…"

40 feet

"What do you mean…how do you know…?"

35 feet

"I just know It won't work. You have to make her stop…" Mr. Vendetta said.

30 feet

"I can't…I don't know how…" Diana said with tears streaming from her face.

25 feet

"Dianaaa!" Steph screamed as she neared the wretched road. Diana felt like she couldn't breathe. Her best friend was going to die because of her.

20 feet

"Yes, you can. Just say it, Diana," Mr. Vendetta said. He focused on her while Diana couldn't take her eyes off Steph.

15 feet

"Say what? I don't know what to say… I can't think. Mr. Vendetta please just *do* something!" Diana said panicking with tears streaming down her face.

10 feet

Steph could hear the cars behind her; Terrified, she yelled "Diana help me!!!!!!"

"You want her to stop walking right? Then tell her," Mr. Vendetta said in a steady voice while placing a hand on her shoulder.

"Okay, stop walking!" Diana screamed with her eyes closed.

5 feet

She opened her eyes to see Mr. Vendetta's disappointed face and Steph still walking. "It didn't work!" Diana yelled.

"You have to feel it. Try again," Mr. Vendetta said.

"Stop walking!" Diana and Mr. Vendetta said in unison.

Steph dropped to her knees, precisely 3 feet away from the road. Diana and Mr. Vendetta ran to her side and helped her up and walked her away from the road.

"Diana…" Steph said.

"Yes, Steph," Diana said.

"Thanks for saving me, I believed in you," Steph said shakily.

"You're welcome…But we are never doing this again," Diana said

"I second that. That was a very dangerous thing you two were doing." Mr. Vendetta said.

"Aww, I was hoping to keep having these near-death experiences," Steph jokingly said.

"What? No? Are you crazy?!" Diana said.

"I'm just kidding, I agree with you," Steph said with a little chuckle.

"Okay good," Diana said with a heavy sigh.

"Oh…and Diana…I didn't mean anything I said. I know your father cared about you. You're a great person. So, how could he not? And I didn't mean-"

"I know," Diana said, interrupting her, pulling her into a tight hug.

"We're best friends. I know you wouldn't hurt me on purpose."

"Just like how I know you won't ever hurt me either," Steph said.

"Okay girls, you all should go home now and don't tell anyone what happened," Mr. Vendetta instructed.

"Our lips are sealed." The girls said in unison as they walked back toward the school.

When the girls finally made it back to the regular part of the school, they said their goodbyes and went to meet their parents at the car rider area... Meanwhile, Tyson had finally made it to his house and his legs stopped moving uncontrollably. Utterly confused, Tyson started to research superpowers on his computer in his room, but of course, only comics and movies showed up from his searches. He decided not to tell his parents because one, they wouldn't believe him and two, just in case they did, he didn't want the government to take Diana away. She was his friend, after all, he just hoped Steph was okay. Tyson laid awake that night hoping and hoping Steph was okay until sleep finally came.

That next morning, he woke up after only getting 5 hours of sleep. He rushed to get ready. He wanted to get to school a bit earlier than he usually did to maybe talk to the janitor to find out what happened to Steph and Diana. When he got downstairs, he warmed up his breakfast in the microwave, left a note for his parents on the fridge like usual, and headed out for school, eating as he walked.

Meanwhile, Diana woke up refreshed, having had a great night's sleep knowing she at least knows how her power works. She just had to learn how to stop it. Her Mom had fixed her an omelet for breakfast and they were off to school.

Steph was pumped that she was still alive when she woke up that morning. Almost dying has a way of making one thankful for life. She hopped out of bed and went to her parent's room and jumped on their bed waking them up. The whole family shared smiles, laughs, and hugs. As Steph walked out the door with her parents to go to school, she wondered what the day had in store for her and her friends. Whatever it was, it surely was going to be anything *but* boring.

CHAPTER 3:

LEARNING CURVE

When Tyson walked through the double doors of the almost empty school, he searched for the janitor. He didn't get a look at his name tag, but he recognized the uniform. When he arrived at Mr. Vendetta's office door with his picture plastered on the side, he knew he found him.

Knock knock!

"Come in," Mr. Vendetta said, pushing aside his papers on his desk.

"You're the guy from yesterday, right?" Tyson asked.

"Yes, that was me," Mr. Vendetta said.

"That's all you have to say? Diana has powers. Which seems like the very same power you have and that's really all you have to say?" Tyson asked, shocked.

"Well, it seems to me you have everything figured out. But I do have a favor to ask of you," Mr. Vendetta said as he walked closer to Tyson.

"It depends on what that favor is," Tyson said.

"Please don't tell Diana about my abilities," Mr. Vendetta said.

"I don't like lying to my friends," Tyson said as he looked down at the ground to avoid Mr. Vendetta's gaze.

"I plan on telling her soon. Please just trust that I know what I'm doing." Mr. Vendetta insisted.

"Okay, it does seem like you're in control of yours. But, you need to pull through on your side of the deal. I won't keep it from her forever and don't use it on me again. Deal?" Tyson asked as he stuck his hand out for Mr. Vendetta to shake.

"Sure," he said, as he shook his hand.

"I really am sorry I had to do that before," Mr. Vendetta.

"I do have one question for you though," Tyson said.

"What is it, young man?" Mr. Vendetta asked.

"How did you know I wouldn't tell on you to my parents when I got home? And my name is Tyson by the way."

"I knew you must have cared about Diana and her friend Stephanie based on your reaction to seeing her power. Also, even if you did, you would have most likely been looked at as crazy, mhm?" Mr. Vendetta explained with a raised brow as he walked toward the door.

"Well, you're right. I do care about my friends and the part about me looking crazy is probably right too." Tyson said with a slight chuckle.

"You should probably go ahead and leave for class. It's almost time for the bell," Mr. Vendetta said as he opened the door.

"Yea I probably should. Bye, Mr. Vendetta," Tyson said as he walked out of the room.

"Bye, Tyson," Mr. Vendetta said as he waved. He watched Tyson walk down the hall and out of his sight before walking back inside his office and closing his door. Mr. Vendetta heavily sighed and got back to work.

Diana's Mom was running late again that morning. So, Diana arrived at school just in time for her to get to class before the bell rang. Once she walked in, she immediately looked for Steph. When their eyes met a smile grew across their faces and they practically ran to each other and hugged. The class, being totally confused about why the girls reacted that way, looked at the two of them weirdly and awkward silence filled the room. Tyson understood the Moment they were sharing but he also knew that if they keep it up then people will start to be suspicious and nosey and that wasn't what they needed right then. So, he said after a dramatic clearing of his throat…

"Umm class is about to start ya'll."

"Oh, right…," Diana and Steph said in unison.

When the girls got to their seats, Mr. Campbell gave them a look of concern and Diana responded with a "don't worry about it" hand motion as he addressed the class.

"Good morning Class. I'm happy to see your smiling faces this morning," Mr. Campbell said.

"Good morning, Mr. Campbell," the class said in unison with a bit of laughter at the pure fallacy of that statement.

"Today we will be learning about citations and why they are so important. Does anyone know what is the use for a citation?" Mr. Campbell asked.

Steph was the first to raise her hand…

"Yes, Stephanie?" Mr. Campbell asked.

"Citations are used to make sure the audience knows where you got your thought from and makes sure the person who created the idea gets their credit," Steph answered.

"That's correct. Citations protect you from committing plagiarism, which is a very big deal that shouldn't be taken lightly. Plagiarism is stealing another's ideas/works and presenting them to others as your very own. That is why I'm going to be discussing the proper way of citing work and when to use citations. Okay, let's get started with this PowerPoint on the Promethean board," Mr. Campbell explained.

While Diana was very happy to see Steph, she couldn't help but think of Mr. Vendetta. "How did he know so much about my power? Does he have it too?! No…no no he can't. He could have just used it to stop Steph versus helping me do it," Diana contemplated in her head. However, she knew she still had to talk to him because he had more information that could help her control her power. Luckily, Diana's Mom was a teacher and taught her everything she needed to know about citations. So, she didn't have to pay too much attention to the PowerPoint which allowed her the chance to daydream about all the scenarios of talking to Mr. Vendetta after school.

Meanwhile...

Steph was distracted by her thoughts about Tyson's unusual reaction to her and Diana having that Moment earlier. Steph liked to read about many things about writing and composition since her dad is an author. She already knew everything about plagiarism. Steph's mind was free to drift off in detective mode during the lesson. "He was acting like he was sympathizing with us for a second. I saw it in his eyes, they were glossy as if he was about to cry too. What does he know?" She contemplated to herself.

When the PowerPoint was over, Mr. Campbell assigned each student a laptop for them to research about tigers and write a 1,000-word essay on them, and include the proper citations. The class seemed to be disappointed in the number of words they would have to write since it would take the remainder of class time to complete, but Diana and Steph loved to write, so they didn't mind. They actually found the assignment to be an exciting challenge. Tyson didn't really care for writing but he was good at it. So, his plan was to get through the essay as fast as possible so he could turn it in early and maybe take a short nap for the rest of the class. The girls finished their assignments early, as expected, but decided to keep writing past the requirement. They didn't have anything better to do. Tyson tried to go to sleep but Mr. Campbell woke him up and gave him another assignment to keep him busy. After the bell rang, Diana quickly gave Steph and Tyson a hug and dashed toward Mr. Vendetta's office. It took her about five minutes to find it but when she did she froze. All the ways this could go wrong started to play out in her head. Mr. Vendetta would see her as a freak and tell on her. She would have to go to a different school *again*. They might even send her to a secret government lab to experiment on her. However, she knew she at least had to try because, if he could help her even a little bit, it would be worth it. The risks of not being able to control her power outweighed everything.

Back in the classroom...

After Diana left the classroom, Steph decided to approach Tyson to see why he seemed *so* understanding.

"Hey, Tyson. I need to ask you something," Steph said while crossing her arms.

"What's up?" Tyson asked while sweat started to form on his forehead. All his secrets came to the forefront of his mind.

"What aren't you telling me?" Steph asked.

"What do you mean?" Tyson asked.

"You were way *too* understanding when Diana and I were hugging. So, what do you know and don't lie to me because I can tell."

"Oh, you have powers too huh?" Tyson said sarcastically.

"So, you do know. You followed us!" Steph said sternly while pointing a finger at him.

"Yeah, I did cause y'all were the ones being suspicious that day and I didn't like how I was left out of it. I thought we were a team. I thought you all trusted me," Tyson said.

"Oh, well...," she didn't know how to respond to that. "Anyway, you shouldn't have followed us," Steph said, tooting her chin up.

"Were you guys ever going to tell me? Or was I going to be left in the dark forever? I thought friends were supposed to trust each other and be there for each other."

"Be there for each other? Where were you when I was about to get hit by a car because things went wrong? You followed us, right? So, you saw everything and didn't want to help me?"

"I... I couldn't help...," Tyson said.

"What do you mean you couldn't help? You could have tried to pull me back or something."

"I could barely hear what's going on...I just kept hearing powers, powers, powers, and her commanding you to do stuff and when you started walking away I froze. I didn't know what to do. I barely knew what was happening. Then, I saw the janitor come and followed behind him from a distance and I saw him rescue you. I'm sorry. I'm sorry I couldn't save you...but y'all should have told me in the first place and then *maybe* I could have really helped because I would have known what was exactly going on." Tyson said with tears welled in his eyes.

"I'm sorry too...for not telling you. We are a team and it isn't fair of me to be upset with you for not helping me when we decided not to tell you about it in the first place. Can we start over?" Steph hopefully questioned with her hand out.

"I did try to help and I was sent home by that janitor," Tyson said in his head.

"Yeah, we can. I'd like that," Tyson said while shaking her hand. Two binding handshakes in one day.

"I'll tell you everything...I'm sure Diana will understand."

As Steph was explaining everything to Tyson, he was able to piece everything together, except how both Diana and Mr. Vendetta have the same power, but he knew he couldn't bring that up now. He had to keep his word. He did feel better, finally being in the know. He demanded to be there when they have another practice, partly because he wanted to help Diana and also to be able to protect Steph in case something goes wrong.

Knock Knock

"Come in," Mr. Vendetta said from his chair.

"Hi, so...umm" Diana mumbled as she walked in.

"You wanna talk about yesterday right?" Mr. Vendetta said, still looking down at his paperwork.

"Yeah. How did you know pulling Steph wouldn't work? How did you know how my power works?" Diana asked.

"You remind me of someone I used to know. He had the same power and it got him in a lot of trouble in his younger days." Mr. Vendetta explained while looking up at her...

"So, there are more people with my power? Can I meet him?" Diana asked excitedly."

"No, I'm afraid I haven't been in contact with him for many years now," Mr. Vendetta said while looking away from Diana's slightly disappointed face that held a bright smile just five seconds earlier.

"Oh...well are there any others you know?" Diana asked, still hopeful.

"No, I don't." Diana immediately looked defeated.

"However, I do know how your power works and how to control it, "Mr. Vendetta quickly added.

"If you'd like for me to help, I-"

"Yes, yes, that would be great!" Diana said, cutting him off.

"Great. Well, I will give you your first lesson," Mr. Vendetta said with a smile to match Diana's.

"Oh okay, I wasn't really prepared but, okay," Diana said hesitantly while shaking her bookbag off her shoulders.

"I don't want you to think of it as a superpower," Mr. Vendetta said, walking around to the front of his desk.

"Why not? It is one right, it can't just be a coincidence?" Diana debated.

"No, it's certainly not a coincidence," Mr. Vendetta said.

"Okay…then…why shouldn't I think of it as a superpower?" Diana asked.

"I don't want you to think of it that way because you have a power that everyone else also has. It's just that your ability has been heightened," Mr. Vendetta said.

"I somewhat understand…I think," Diana said. Mr. Vendetta could see the confusion still present on her face.

"You see, everyone's words have power. However, most of the time the power of their words affects others' emotional and mental state, but *your* words can affect their mental, emotional, and physical state." Mr. Vendetta further explained.

"Okay, I get it now. That seems like a lot of…"

"Responsibility? Yes, it is. Even though sometimes it may seem like a burden, it is, in fact, a gift and you should cherish it," Mr. Vendetta said.

"So, how does it work exactly? The physical part doesn't always happen when I say something," Diana asked.

"We will get to that on another day. I assume your Mom will be here shortly to pick you up," Mr. Vendetta said.

"Yeah, she is. How did you know?" Diana asked.

"I'm the school janitor. I notice everything haha…Even the escapade in the cafeteria the other day," Mr. Vendetta explained.

"You saw that too?! How come you didn't help sooner?" Diana asked.

"I had to be sure. This isn't something you want everyone to know about. This also includes your mother. No one must know about your powers." Mr. Vendetta insisted.

"Well, Steph already knows but, I won't tell anyone else."

"Okay good. And there's one more thing I want you to do," Mr. Vendetta said.

"Okay, what is it?" Diana asked

"I want you to sign up for the Debate Team. I'll explain later but you have to sign up today because they are going to take the sign-up sheet down tomorrow morning," Mr. Vendetta said.

"Okay, I do like to argue. I'll make sure to sign up today," Diana said with a thumbs up.

"Alright, well you better get going. We'll talk soon," Mr. Vendetta said with a little chuckle.

"Bye, Mr. Vendetta!" Diana said as she picked up her book bag and walked out the door.

"Bye, Diana," Mr. Vendetta said as he waved.

As soon as Diana walked out the door, she saw Steph sitting in crisscross applesauce up against the wall.

"How did you know I'd be here?" Diana said with a smirk.

"What can I say, I know you well," Steph said with a little chuckle.

"Let's walk and talk cause my Mom is going to be here soon," Diana said, helping Steph off the floor.

"Okay… but I've been waiting, so what did he say?! What did you'll talk about?" Steph asked excitedly.

"He said he'd basically be my mentor. He knew someone a while ago with my power and he figured out how it works and is going to teach me," Diana explained.

"That's great, you have your own Yoda, young sky walker," Steph said.

"Haha, but he did teach me one thing," Diana said.

"What was it…was it like super deep?" Steph said.

"Yeah it was actually. Oh, he told me to sign up for the debate team before it gets taken down tomorrow," Diana said while she walked to the board and signed her name.

"That sounds fun and I figured that. That's why I'm going to call him Yoda from now on." Steph said.

"He said that I don't have superpowers. In fact, I have a power that everyone else has as well. Mine is heightened and is a gift," Diana said.

"Ohh, I get it. Like my words have power too I just can't make anyone do anything I tell them like you," Steph said.

"Yeah, that's basically it. Your words can hurt people's feelings and affect their thoughts and mine can do that and affect what their body does too," Diana explained.

"Oh, so I have power too, cool," Steph said while nodding her head.

"Yeah, I never thought of it that way before," Diana said while opening the double doors.

When the girls stepped outside, they scanned the cars lined up outside the school and Diana saw her Mom near the front right behind Steph's Dad.

"I'll see you tomorrow, Steph," Diana said while running to the car.

"Bye, see ya!" Steph said, running to her Dad's truck.

When Diana got into the car, her Mom started their usual after-school conversation and after it was over, Diana went ahead and told her about joining the debate team. Her Mom was concerned that she was taking on too much with being in the Art Club and Debate Team. Diana was able to convince her she could handle it. So, her mother said she would support her as long as it didn't interfere with her studies since that should be the most important thing she should be concerned about. Ms. Monroe trusted that Diana knew herself and knew what she could handle and couldn't wait until she could see her do her thing at her first debate competition. To show Diana how excited she was, Ms. Monroe took her out to Red Lobster. Diana could already taste the mouthwatering shrimp scampi and cheddar biscuits. She ran out of the car when they arrived. When Diana and Ms. Monroe got home, Diana was determined to make her Mom proud and decided she would fully dedicate herself to working extremely hard to be the best debater she could be. She went ahead and looked up the rules of debate on her Mom's laptop before she had her first official meeting next Wednesday. That night, Diana researched until sleep overcame her.

Each night, for a week straight, Diana researched to make sure she was fully prepared for her first meeting and it was almost time for her to show just how much she learned. The meeting was set for 4:00 pm and Diana could only pay attention to the clock tick away. Steph noticed it and decided to take extra detailed notes so that way she could give them to Diana after class so she wouldn't get behind. She knew Diana was a worrier. Tyson apparently had the same idea because, after class both he and Steph went up to Diana with their notes ready to hand to her.

"Aww, thanks, guys. You guys are the best. I'll use them both," Diana said smiling looking at both of their papers.

"Oh well, Steph's is probably better," Tyson said while scratching behind his neck and blushing.

"I'm still taking them both," Diana insisted while watching Steph turn away smiling.

"I hope you have fun at the meeting today. I know you will do well," Steph said.

"Yeah, do great," Tyson added.

"Thanks, guys. I hope all the time I spent researching paid off. Bye, see y'all tomorrow," Diana said as she left the classroom.

"See ya," Tyson and Steph said in unison while waving.

Diana's nerves were on ten as she walked to the library where the meeting would take place. Even though it was only 3:30 pm, Diana still went ahead and sat at the round table to wait for everyone to get there. As she sat there, she wondered how the meeting would go, if the team members were going to be nice, if they were going to talk about strategy, if they were going to create teams; Diana pondered this for a while until kids started to show up. She recognized a few faces from seeing them in the hallway but had never talked to them, but she was optimistic. She just had experienced a sense of relief until Hannah walked into the room and sat down a few seats away from her. Diana hoped she was there by chance and maybe needed a book and was waiting on the librarian, but she knew that was just wishful thinking. However, she knew she couldn't back out simply because a girl she wasn't fond of was part of the club. She had to be more mature, she was in the middle after all. The teacher who was over the club, Mr. Kyle, seemed really nice and quirky which made Diana more at ease.

"Alright everyone, today will just be about getting to know one another and toward the end, I will give each of you your topic to write your debating speech for, okay?"

"Okay's," filled the room.

"Alrighty then. First things first, everyone state your name, grade, and favorite hobby. Let's start over here," Mr. Kyle instructed as he pointed to a boy three seats away from Diana.

Diana didn't even catch the people's names or hobbies before her because all she could do was figure out her answer and keep repeating in her head until it was her turn to make sure she was prepared. She was so focused on thinking about what she was going to say that Mr. Kyle had to clap to get her attention when it was finally her turn.

Diana, feeling a tad bit embarrassed, said: "Hi, my name is Diana. I'm in the sixth grade, and my favorite hobby is meditating," After she was done, the other kids looked intrigued and that made Diana feel good because she didn't want to be looked at as boring. Finally, she could finally pay attention to the other kid's introductions. Everyone had something interesting to say. Diana could tell these were good people, but then it was Hannah's turn... cue eye roll. "Hello, my name is Hannah. I'm in the seventh grade and I like to draw," she said. Diana liked to draw as well. "Maybe there is more to Hannah than what I thought, maybe I should give her another chance. Maybe she was having a bad day," Diana thought to herself. After the last kid said their introduction, Mr. Kyle handed everyone a sheet of paper that contained their perspective of the topic, for the preservation of the shark species or for the extinction of the shark species.

"There will be a mock competition in a few months to hopefully give you all insight for the real competition that will take place towards the end of the year. Students like Jake, Hannah, and Drew are a few members who took part in the school's competition last year and would be more than willing to help you all out," Mr. Kyle explained.

"Maybe I can ask Hannah for some help after the meeting is over," Diana thought.

"Okay, I will give you all about ten minutes to look over your topic and you may talk amongst each other about them before I dismiss everyone for today's meeting. Remember we will meet every Tuesday and Thursday promptly at 4:00pm," Mr. Kyle announced.

Diana decided to stay to herself, after seeing that a good bit of the other students already knew each other and started talking and looked over her topic. "For the preservation of the shark species, this will be interesting," she read aloud. Ten minutes went by quickly. Diana got up from her chair and went out into the hallway to wait on Hannah to come out and ask her for advice. Diana was experiencing a lot of anxiety, but she was determined to give Hannah another shot.

What she didn't know is that Mr. Vendetta was nearby taking the garbage out of the neighboring classroom. Hannah was the last person to leave.

"Hey, Hannah," Diana said shyly as Hannah walked out the library.

"What do you want?" Hannah asked as she kept walking.

"Well...I was wondering if you could give me some advice?" Diana asked while following close behind her. Hannah stopped and turned around to look directly at Diana.

"Yeah, I'll give you some advice. You should stop now before you embarrass yourself later. You won't even make it past the mock debate," Hannah replied.

"Wow...and I really thought you might have just had a bad day and that *maybe* because we both liked to draw we could possibly get along but I see that's not the case with you," Diana said.

"You really thought just because we have one thing in common I would want to be *your* friend. You're a pathetic underclassman," Hannah said.

"You're only one grade higher than me, you don't have much of an upper hand on me," Diana replied.

"Oh, but I'm the girl who won last year's debating competition, I'm the girl who is the best looking, I'm the girl who gets what she wants," Hannah said.

"You can't always get what you want, you know. Someday you won't, and that's life," Diana replied. Hannah laughed.

"Who told you that? Your Mommy? Is that the excuse she gives you when you can't get what you want? Is that why you don't have any nice clothes or shoes? I will always get my way, best believe I will," Hannah said while starting to walk away.

"Why do you have to be so mean to people? Don't you know you can hurt people's feelings?!" Diana asked as her frustration began to show on her face.

"Aww did I hurt little Diana's feelings? I don't care. Hurting your or anyone for that matter means nothing to me, it doesn't affect me at all," Hannah said.

"How can you be so careless?! You're a terrible person and I hope you feel tenfold what you've brought upon others," Diana said

"Whatev-" Hannah said as she suddenly stopped walking with tears swelling in her eyes.

"What's wrong with me? My chest hurts...What's going on?" Hannah muttered.

"It must be karma," Diana said as she walked away leaving Hannah crying in the hallway.

As she walked past the room Mr. Vendetta was in, Mr. Vendetta hung his head low. When Diana got to her Mom's car, part of her felt great that Hannah got what she deserved and the other part of her felt bad that she made her cry and her chest hurt. She knew her power must have kicked in and she desperately tried to convince herself for the rest of the night that she made the right decision. In the end, she decided to get to school early the next day to talk to Mr. Vendetta. "Maybe he can make me feel better about it," she thought.

It was the next morning and the sun hadn't risen yet. Diana woke her Mom up to tell her she had to get to school early to help her teacher set up some stuff and even though her Mom was upset she waited till the very last minute to give her that information, she went ahead and got up. They were able to leave the house early enough to get to her school in time to talk to Mr. Vendetta. Once Diana reached Mr. Vendetta's door, she immediately knew he most likely wasn't going to ease her conscience.

Knock Knock

"Come in," Mr. Vendetta said.

"Hi. Umm," Diana muttered. She walked in and closed the door.

"I know why you're here…" Mr. Vendetta said as he made his way around his desk toward Diana.

"You do?" Diana said with her head down.

"I heard everything…And I'm very disappointed in you Diana," Mr. Vendetta said with a sigh.

"But why me? When she's the-"

"Do you think she deserved the intense chest pain and sadness you just gave her possibly for the rest of the day? Are you proud of that?" Mr. Vendetta asked sternly, cutting Diana off.

"But she hurt me first. She basically called me ugly and pathetic," Diana said definitively while clutching the straps of her book bag.

"And that deems you worthy to hurt her? I actually know that young lady and what has gone through and it isn't what you'd think. She doesn't put on makeup because she likes it she puts it on because if she didn't her scars would show. I've seen her place the powdery stuff on her arms and neck to hide them." Mr. Vendetta said.

"Her parents are hurting her?!" Diana asked with wide eyes.

"No, Ms. Brown was adopted. Her first family abused her and she was taken away. Her new family barely acknowledges her, they just give her whatever she wants to keep her quiet and they are barely home. I know you've heard this before but it's true. Hurt people hurt people. So, you have to-"

"Be the bigger person cause I'm better than she is," Diana said, cutting him off.

"No that's not it either. No one, no matter what they've done, accomplished, or haven't done is better than anyone else. Someone can do better at a skill than you but that doesn't make them actually better than you. Skills can be worked on whether it's wits, strength, or endurance; they can get better if you work at them. However, in the category of being a human being, no one is simply better than anyone else. All you can do is boost your attributes to the highest level possible and be the best person you possibly can without comparing yourself to anyone else. Only your definition of what it means to be a good person at heart is the one that actually matters. You can't compare yourself to others, you should only compare yourself to your old self. You have to focus on yourself, the kind of person you want to be, the person you wish to become. Do you want to be a person who hurts people?" Mr. Vendetta asked.

"No, but she hurt me first. It's more like self-defense. It's not like I knew I was going to actually make her be in pain or really sad or what she's been through in her life. All I did was make her feel what she makes everyone else feel. How she made *me* feel. Plus, I don't really know how my powers work," Diana said while crossing her arms and looking anywhere else but at his face.

"It doesn't matter if you don't know the terms and conditions of your powers yet. The first thing I taught you was that your words, like everyone else's, have power and you have to heed to that responsibility. You did not heed that responsibility. The second you used your power to hurt her you became the girl who hurt someone. Is that who you want to be, is that who you are?" Mr. Vendetta asked.

"No, it isn't," Diana replied.

"Exactly." Mr. Vendetta said.

"So, what can I do when I get really upset if it happens again?" Diana asked inquisitively.

"You can use your power on yourself," Mr. Vendetta replied.

"So, start telling myself to calm down? I don't know if I can do that without people thinking something is wrong with me," Diana said.

"No, not that. I'm going to teach you about what I like to call defensive affirmations," Mr. Vendetta said.

"Defensive affirmations? That sounds like football," Diana said.

"Well...it isn't but that's a nice correlation. It is something I made up that has helped me in the past when I've been in similar situations, of course not with the power you have, but still similar. Instead of directing the focus of your comebacks at her, direct it toward yourself. I'll give you an example. Call me an ugly old man," Mr. Vendetta instructed.

"But I don't think you're an ugly old man," Diana said.

"It's just an exercise, I know you don't mean it," Mr. Vendetta said as he gestured for Diana to sit down.

"Okay...you're an ugly old man."

"I am a beautiful man and your words won't affect me." Mr. Vendetta said.

"I don't understand. I thought you said *everyone's* words have power. So, wouldn't her words still hurt me if she said that even if it is to a smaller degree than the way my words would affect her? And I'm supposed to say that back?" Diana asked.

"Yes, that's true but we as humans also have the power to make ourselves feel better. When you get a paper cut what happens in a few days?" Mr. Vendetta asked.

"It heals," Diana said.

"Yes, if physical wounds can heal then so can emotional wounds. Just like how your body can do it on its own even if sometimes it's a really deep wound. It would just take the body a while to completely heal. It is the same way you can make yourself feel better by using the power of your own words. End every defensive affirmation with your words will not affect me even if they have already. It's almost like a fight with words, where the other person is throwing punches, and instead of you fighting back, you use your own shield to deflect their attacks. And if the shield breaks with a harsh attack then you rebuild it tougher and more durable the next time." Mr. Vendetta said.

"I think I get it now," Diana said with a slight nod.

"Okay, so if a person was to say "you're weird and pathetic", what would be your defensive affirmation?" Mr. Vendetta asked Diana.

"I would say 'I'm awesome and your words will not affect me," Diana replied

"That's it. You got it. So, always remember that. You don't have to try and hurt everyone who hurts you. You can protect yourself and protect your energy by focusing on yourself and leaving them alone with their impolite opinions," Mr. Vendetta said.

But, what should I do about Hannah?" Diana asked.

"What's been done has already been done. Sadly, you can never take back what you say emotionally. People will always remember how you make them feel even if they can't remember what you said," Mr. Vendetta said.

"I'm confused again," Diana said.

"Okay, I'll put it this way. You know how you were able to save Steph by using your words to undo what you had said before. You can say something to someone and then right after you tell them you didn't mean it and you're sorry, thus physically taking the words back but not emotionally. You will never be able to take back the feeling you gave her when you said those words. That's why you must be aware of what you're saying and ask yourself if you really mean it before you say it, especially when you are emotionally involved yourself," Mr. Vendetta explained.

"You mean when I get angry?" Diana asked.

Yes, when you get angry, or upset in any way really," Mr. Vendetta replied.

"Yeah, people have told me that I have some anger issues," Diana said. "No, there's no such thing as anger issues, there is nothing wrong with you. You simply get emotionally involved with things quicker and more easily than others that doesn't have to be a bad thing. You just have to find a way to ease yourself. That is why I wanted you to join the debate team. Doing that kind of work will test you because you get emotionally invested in your own perspective and it's up to you to be able to control your power."

"Oh...so that's why you wanted me to join. I guess that makes sense. It's also a bit scary. But when you say at ease do you mean calm down?" Diana asked.

"Somewhat, it's more of knowing yourself and what you need at that moment and doing it to make yourself feel better, and plus I know you can handle it. You are a very smart young lady," Mr. Vendetta said.

"Well if you're about to say count down from ten then I should tell you that never works for me, usually, because the person who caused me to get upset picks on me because I'm doing it and it messes me up and I get mad all over again," Diana said.

"Well, there is something else you could do when you can't physically get away from a situation. You can go inside your head for a Moment, take a second to gather yourself."

"Alright, you're confusing me yet again. What does 'going into my head' mean?" Diana asked.

"You can use your imagination."

"Isn't that just for little kids?" Diana asked.

"No, you're never too old to have an active imagination."

"So, I'm just going to imagine myself getting calmer and it'll happen?" Diana asked, looking very skeptical.

"Umm no, not at all. Where is a place that makes you feel peaceful?" Mr. Vendetta asked.

"I like my room," Diana replied.

"Well, what part of your room do you like the most?" Mr. Vendetta asked.

"I like the stars on my ceiling and my comfy pillows and stuffed animals on my bed," Diana replied. She started smiling just thinking about it.

"What do you hear when you're in there?" Mr. Vendetta asked.

"I hear nothing, blissful silence," Diana replied.

"What do you smell?" Mr. Vendetta asked.

"I smell the lavender scent from my air freshener my Mom puts in my room," Diana replied.

"How do you feel right now?" Mr. Vendetta asked.

"I... I feel...calm," Diana said excitedly.

"So, the next time you get upset, go into your head into your room and think about the touch of the stuffed animals and pillows around you. Think of the lavender scent you smell. And picture yourself looking up at the stars on your ceiling. And most of all, tune out all the noise around you and listen for your blissful silence. Practice doing this at home so your ability to create this reality gets faster and faster. So, in real-life situations, it won't take you too long to gather yourself if an altercation were to arise," Mr. Vendetta said

"Hey, this reminds me of meditating. I like to meditate sometimes when there's just a lot going on," Diana said.

"It should, it is just like meditating but instead of clearing your mind, you are going to construct a memory that gives you a feeling of peace. Then, you will feel calm and go back to the situation with a more leveled head because you work best when you're calm," Mr. Vendetta explained.

"Hey, that's what my Mom says too," Diana said.

"Well……she gives good advice," Mr. Vendetta said.

"And so, do you, I'm going to practice and try that next time," Diana said.

"Alright well, I have to start on my cleaning, or I will lose my job and you have to get to class before the bell rings. So, have a great day, Okay? Oh, and I didn't tell you about Hannah's situation so you could tell others now…" Mr. Vendetta said.

"You won't have to worry about that, my lips are sealed. Bye, Mr. Vendetta!" Diana yelled as she walked out of the room.

"Bye Diana," Mr. Vendetta said as he started to get up and grab his tools.

Later that day, at home, Diana did a lot of meditation and self-reflection and decided that she would apologize to Hannah the next day. She didn't know how exactly she would apologize for something she's not allowed to tell her she did, but she knew she had to do something. Even though Mr. Vendetta told her to leave it alone, it wasn't sitting right with her not to do anything after she hurt someone even if it wasn't exactly on purpose. To try and distract herself, she started researching her debating topic.

Since Diana was a lover of animals, she was drawn to trying to debate on the half of sharks being essential rather than a burden. She researched until her eyes drooped and eventually fell asleep.

It was the next morning and Diana still hadn't figured what it was that she would say to Hannah, after much contemplation she decided she figured she'd just let the words come to her. In the car she was anxious, but she tried to do what Mr. Vendetta said about going into her head, into her room, to see if that would make her feel better in this situation too and it did, not as much as she hoped but it did help some. She never got tired of passing that Pedita Middle School sign with the intertwined vines wrapped around it, she felt like she belonged and was meant to be there. That thought put her at ease too. When she got inside those double doors she met up with Steph and Tyson by the class door.

"Hey, guys!" Diana said.

"Hey!" Steph and Tyson said in unison.

"How was your first debate team practice?" Steph asked excitedly.

"Oh...umm it was good. The teacher was funny," Diana replied as she scratched her neck.

"That's great," Tyson said.

"Yeah...totally," Steph said.

"So...um where is Mr. Campbell today? He still isn't here yet?" Diana asked.

"No, he isn't here, maybe he's in traffic or something. I'll go ask Mr. Vendetta if he can let us in so we can sit down," Tyson replied as he walked away.

"Okay," Diana said.

"I know something happened yesterday...Don't worry, you don't have to tell me. You're your own person and don't have to tell me everything. I trust that you know I'll be here for you if you do need me though or if you would like to tell me what's going on, I'll listen," Steph said.

"Thanks, Steph," Diana said as she gave Steph a huge hug. She really needed to hear those words.

"Aww dang...why do I always miss the hugs?" Tyson asked, accompanied by Mr. Vendetta unlocking the door.

"Get in here," Diana said as she pulled him into their hug.

"Hey, I need to know if you all will be available to meet with me tomorrow after school so we can discuss things," Mr. Vendetta insisted.

"Sure, I'm free," Diana replied.

"So am I," Steph said.

"I'm in," Tyson said.

"Okay, great. I will see you all tomorrow have a good day," Mr. Vendetta said as he walked away, looking at them as they waved at him.

When all the students entered the classroom, they talked amongst themselves until Mr. Campbell showed up. It took him about ten minutes to get there. "I'm sorry I'm late everyone. There was an accident on the expressway and I had to take back streets to get here. I hope you all had a good chat because today I will be assigning a team project on different habitats that will be due in four days," Mr. Campbell explained. The students in the class seemed to be excited about the project and of course, Diana, Steph, and Tyson immediately started looking at one another insinuating their partnership.

During class, Mr. Campbell talked about what exactly a biome is, what characteristics make up certain biomes, and how different species of animals and plants adapt and survive in them. Since Diana was so captivated by the lesson she was shocked when she heard the bell signaling their lunch-time. When Diana walked into the cafeteria with Steph and Tyson at her side, she scanned the endless rows of students to look for Hannah. However, she spotted her at the table for silent lunch so she decided she would give her the apology later.

"So, are you as excited about the project as I am?" Steph asked.

"Definitely, I didn't really want the lesson to end, but we have to eat soo…" Diana replied.

"I wouldn't say I'm excited, but I think the project will be fun. I wonder what exactly he will make us do," Tyson responded.

"I do too. I think he will probably assign each team a biome and make us do another presentation." Steph said.

"I think it might be more to it, only because we could do that in one class. We don't need four days to complete it," Diana said.

"Yeah, that's true. I guess we will find out when we get back," Steph said.

When they got back to class, Mr. Campbell finished his PowerPoint presentation and handed everyone a worksheet explaining the project. It said that each group has to prepare a poster illustrating a certain biome of their choice as well as write a 1,000-word essay talking about their biome and a PowerPoint presentation that would go along with the poster to present to the class. All of it was definitely a whole day's worth of work but Diana was still excited since the topic was at least appealing to her.

At the end of class, Diana, Steph, and Tyson got together to discuss a day for them to all get together to maybe knock out a good bit of the assignment and to just chill with each other since they haven't hung out outside of school. Steph offered her place for them to meet up since she knew her parents loved company.

Since Tyson wasn't a really artsy person, he chose to be the one to write the essay since, he said, "I would get a chance to sleep and take it easy until the presentation after I'm done." Diana chose the PowerPoint since she was tech-savvy which left Steph with completing the poster. Once that was settled they went their separate ways; Tyson to the walkers and Steph to the car-riders pick up area and Diana pretending to go to the bathroom but really hoping to find Hannah to apologize to her before her Mother gets there.

Diana went over to the 7th graders' hall in hopes of finding Hannah and spotted her at her locker. Diana thought the seventh and eighth graders having lockers while 6th graders didn't was unfair but understandable since they had to switch to more classes than them. However, she set that thought aside and calmed down, and started walking toward Hannah hoping something would actually come out of her mouth.

"Hi, Hannah. I just wanted to say I'm sorry. I didn't-"

"Just do me a favor and leave me alone. I don't know why my stomach started hurting after you yelled at me, but it was freaky and I don't really wanna be around you. So, you stay in your lane and I'll stay in mine. Got it?" Hannah asked, interrupting her.

"Okay…," Diana replied

"Good," Hannah said as she strutted down the hallway.

"Wow, well that went better than I hoped it would. She does make it really hard for me to try and be nice to her, but us not paying each other attention seems like a great idea," Diana thought to herself as she walked back to the car-riders area. She knew that what Hannah said was actually good advice, that she should just be focusing on herself and being the best person, debater, student, and friend, she could be instead of worrying about people that don't care about her and what they have to say. That night, Diana completed her homework and watched a movie with her Mom, *Trolls*. *Trolls* was Diana's favorite movie, it always put everything in a different, brighter perspective and boosted her spirit. Diana went to sleep with happy thoughts and dreamed away.

The next day, Diana woke up refreshed and her mind raced with thoughts of what Mr. Vendetta was going to tell them. She wondered if he maybe had some major news, maybe if he had found out there were others like her. She let her mind entertain the thought for a second and then decided to shut it out because she didn't want to dwell on that thought for too long just in case that wasn't the case. She didn't want to give herself false hope. When she got to school, everything went like any other day with Mr. Campbell rambling about a topic that in this case was multiplying fractions to the terrible school lunch all the way up until it was time for the school bell to ring.

Ding! Ding!

Diana was ready to just jump out of her seat, grab Tyson and Steph, and run to Mr. Vendetta's office. However, she kept her composer and settled on a huge smile across her face as she walked to them. Tyson looked concerned but figured it couldn't be a bad thing since she was indeed smiling. Steph knew she was excited about something, but couldn't figure out what it was.

"Are y'all ready to go talk to Mr. Vendetta?" Diana asked the two of them.

"Yeah, are you okay Diana? I've never seen you smile that much," Steph asked with a happily confused look.

"Yeah...I noticed that too. I just wasn't going to say anything about it but yeah what is going on with you?" Tyson added.

"I'm just excited about what Mr. Vendetta might be telling us. I mean think about it, he is bringing all of us together for something. So, it must be something huge like maybe he found some other people like me, like think about how great that could be." Diana was just bubbling with excitement of all the possibilities.

"Yeeaaah…. or just hear me out now. He might just want to really tell us about your powers. Has he even explained exactly how your powers work?" Steph asked.

"Well…no he hasn't…I guess you're right," Diana said as her smile fell.

"Hey, that's still something important you need to know and it would help you a lot. It still is something to be excited for," Tyson said.

"Yeah you've been wondering how your powers work for a while now," Steph added.

"Don't let that *whole* smile go away. Just a little bit of it so you don't look creepy," Tyson said as he chuckled, causing a smile to slowly creep back on Diana's face.

"Thanks guys. Okay, we should go now. We don't want to keep him waiting," Diana said.

When they got to Mr. Vendetta's door Diana knocked lightly and he let them in. He had been expecting them…

"Hello, kids. I wanted to talk to you all about Diana's powers, how they work, and how you can help her," Mr. Vendetta explained.

"Okay," Diana said as her smile faded a bit.

"Alright, so first things first. Diana, your powers are tied to your emotions and I don't just mean anger. Anger and fear are the emotions that takes your powers to its fullest strength. However, sadness, happiness, and more also serve as an amplifier for your powers. I know I've told this to you before Diana, but I want to make sure you know that while everyone also has the power that affects others' mental and emotional states your power also amplifies your effect on others' mental and emotional states more than regular people. Do you understand Diana?" Mr. Vendetta asked.

"Yes, I believe I do...that means I really have to watch what I say huh? Diana asked.

"No, you don't have to necessarily watch what you say. You have to be aware of what you are saying. You have to make sure, especially in situations where your emotions are intense, that you mean what you say and are prepared for what comes after. Always understand that some things don't need to be said at all and that there are many effective ways to say what you need to say without being mean and disrespectful."

"Oh okay. I was taught to do that anyway. "If you don't have something nice to say don't say it all'," Diana recited.

"Yes, that's very true but I would like to add on that also. If it is not relevant, then you also don't have to say anything. There will be times where maybe it won't be considered a nice thing to say, but it needs to be said and then you should say it, just make sure you adjust how you say it to still be respectful. However, those Moments will be interpreted by you, it will be your call and I trust that you will choose wisely."

"I'll do the best I can," Diana said.

"I know...Now for you Tyson and Steph, you guys as Diana's close friends are able to help her," Mr. Vendetta said.

"How?!" Steph said before Tyson could even say anything.

"Well...your powers are weaker than Diana's and don't necessarily affect another person physically, but since you have a close bond with Diana think of it as your powers being amplified with strength due to your bond, so much so that you can affect her mentally and emotionally in a way that would highly influence her actions."

"That's cool!" Tyson said.

"Yeah, you see it all the time on tv when a person is about to do something wrong and someone gets a person that is close to them to tell them not to do it, hoping they would be able to get through to them and stop them. I didn't know that we could do it for Diana since she actually has powers," Steph said.

"Well, it can work. It may take some extra effort, but you could get her to stop doing something because she cares about you all and what you both have to say," Mr. Vendetta explained.

"We can be like her protectors, you know, just like from herself," Tyson said.

"Yes, but remember that the most important thing is your friendship because that is what's going to ensure you all will be able to continue to be her protector," Mr. Vendetta said,

"Then we definitely have this in the bag," Steph said while giving Tyson a high five.

"Aww thanks guys," Diana said.

"No problem, we will always be there for you," Tyson said with one of the biggest grins she'd ever seen him do.

"That's all I have for you all today. You all are very intelligent and good people so I know you'll work hard to keep the secret and make sure to protect each other," Mr. Vendetta said. It warmed his heart to see how they were all ready to take on this challenge.

"We will," they said in unison as they started walking out.

Tyson had walked Diana and Steph to the car rider's area and he proceeded to walk his daily route home. The walk used to feel really long for him but as the days continued it got easier and easier for him to complete it. When he got home, he was met with yet another note on the freezer stating, "There's dinner in the fridge," with a smiley face. Tyson liked these messages his Mom would leave him. He missed them during the day, but he had grown adjusted to being by himself, alone in the house. He had been alone in the house ever since the 3rd grade. He never truly felt lonely though. He enjoyed his own company and liked to build different contraptions in his spare time. His parents were doctors, who saved lives every day, so he never resented his parents for leaving him alone in the house. He had asked them last night if they thought they could get Uncle Jeffery to pick him up after school to take him to

Steph's house. They said they would try to and that if he doesn't see his car then he would need to catch a ride with Steph or Diana. After he ate his dinner, later that night he pondered about his new role, the protector… he liked the way that sounded.

However, he couldn't help but to think about when Mr. Vendetta was going to tell Diana about his powers. It made him feel bad for keeping that from Diana and Steph. "How would they think of me if they found out I knew all along? Would they understand that I was just trying to be respectful to Mr. Vendetta's wishes and that I really wanted him to tell Diana *or* would they view me as a traitor and cast me out of the group? How can I call myself her protector if I am lying to them?… That's it. I'm going to tell Mr. Vendetta that he has until next week to tell Diana or I will," Tyson thought to himself. That night, Tyson drifted off to sleep with anticipation in his heart for whatever was coming ahead for him and his friends.

It's the next day and Steph wakes up excited about Diana and Tyson coming over. Her Dad said he is going to fix them some of his famous finger sandwiches which made Steph even more excited for their arrival. On the way to the school, Steph was wondering if Mr. Campbell would allow the groups to get together to talk about their project and updates and things of that nature. She knew that her group had already established a plan, but she honestly just wanted an excuse for them to talk and chill a bit in class.

When she arrived at school she saw Diana and Tyson waiting at the door.

"Hey Steph, Mr. Campbell must be late again today," Diana said.

"Hopefully he gets here soon, maybe they'll send Mr. Vendetta to let us in so we won't have to stand outside for too long."

"They probably- and there he is walking right toward us along with some lady," Diana said.

"Maybe it's our substitute," Steph said.

"Yeah, most likely she is," Diana said.

"Tyson, you're pretty quiet today, are you okay?" Steph asked.

"Oh…I'm fine. I'm just in my own world…," Tyson said.

Steph thought he was lying or at least not telling the whole truth, but she didn't want to push it. On another note, Steph was right about that lady being the substitute teacher. Her name was Ms. Worcester and she was a very sweet old lady. She read off the instruction left to her by Mr. Campbell very slowly to the class so that they would all know what was expected of them and informed them that if they were to finish their assignments early they could talk to their group about their project. This made the students really happy because they had the opportunity to be able to talk to each other. So, everyone in the class started working on their work with a quickness to make sure they could get as long as possible to be able to talk later.

After lunch had ended and everyone got back to class, almost everyone was done with their assignments and the conversing started.

"So, are you guys ready to work on the project at my house? My Dad is going to make finger sandwiches!" Steph said excitedly.

"Yeah, I am and what's the difference between them and regular sandwiches other than the sides?" Diana asked.

"Well, nothing really, but my Dad has his special sauce he puts on them that makes it taste sooo good. I can't wait," Steph said.

"It must not be something he makes often then, huh?" Diana asked, giggling at Steph's excitement.

"No, the sauce takes a long time to make so he usually only cooks them when we have company over or for some special occasion," Steph explained.

"Well, I can't wait to try them. What about you, Tyson?" Diana asked, trying to bring him into the conversation.

"Oh...umm...Yeah, I'm ready to try them," Tyson replied.

"Alrighty then...Have you guys already started working on the project?" Steph asked.

"I have the color schemes, transitions, and the general topics for each slide so far," Diana responded

"Okay, Tyson?" Steph asked.

"I made a general outline for the essay and I brought my laptop to start and hopefully finish at your house," Tyson answered.

"Okay good, I bought all the paint for the poster and border letters. Hopefully, I'll finish later today too," Steph said.

The bell rang signaling for Steph, Tyson, and Diana to all walk to the car rider area. Diana's Mom was parked near the school sign and Steph's Dad was, coincidentally, right behind her waiting on Steph.

They all walked to the cars and Steph introduced her Dad to Ms. Monroe and he gave her their address. Then, Tyson pulls Diana to the side.

"Hey, umm do you think I can ride with y'all, my uncle is not here to take me?" Tyson asked shyly.

"Yeah, we can take you. My Mom doesn't like last-minute things, but she won't just let you walk there or not be able to come," Diana said.

"Thanks, I'm sorry it's so last minute," Tyson said.

"You're good. I'll go tell my Mom," Diana said.

"Okay," Tyson said nervously. It was his first time meeting her Mom.

"Hey Mom, can Tyson ride with us to Steph's house?" Diana asked with a wide smile.

"Now you know- Why are you just *now* asking me? Are his parents okay with this?" Ms. Monroe asked.

"Yes, they said he could," Diana replied.

"Okay, I'll take him. Does he have a ride home?" Ms. Monroe asked.

"I highly doubt it, he walks home every day after school," Diana said.

"His parents don't have a car?" Ms. Monroe asked.

"No, I'm quite sure that they do. They are big-time doctors and are always at the hospital working," Diana said.

"Well bless his heart, being alone all the time. That poor baby," Ms. Monroe said.

"He says he's okay with being alone because he knows they are needed at the hospital for saving lives," Diana says while looking back at Tyson once again being lost in his own world.

"That's a great attitude to have. I'm glad he has you and Steph to keep him company though," Ms. Monroe said.

"I am too. He's a great friend," Diana said.

"Alright then, go ahead and tell him to come on so we can follow Steph's Dad because you know me and directions...," Ms. Monroe said with a chuckle.

"Haha...Okay," Diana said as she waved to him to come on over.

"Are you guys ready to get going?" Steph's Dad asked.

"Ready!" Steph, Diana, and Tyson said in unison.

"Then let's go," Ms. Monroe said as she got in the car.

On the way there, Diana expected Tyson to not say much, but literally all he said was," Thank you for taking me," to Ms. Monroe.

The ride wasn't too long but Tyson was already knocked out by the time they reached Steph's house. Luckily, he wasn't difficult to wake up.

Steph's house was beautiful. There were flowers everywhere and when they walked inside it felt cool and cozy. When Diana and Tyson walked in, they automatically smelt what they expected was the sauce for the finger sandwiches and they drooled in their mouths.

"You smell that...It's the sauce Ahhh?!" Steph asked.

"It smells delicious. I'm really excited to try it now," Diana replied.

"Yeah me too," Tyson added.

"I'll bring you all the sandwiches in about an hour, that'll give you guys enough time to at least start with the project, right?" Steph's Dad said as he walked past us to the kitchen.

"Yes, that will be okay. Thank you," Steph answered.

"Alrighty then," he replied.

"Okay, guys the living room is this way, follow me," Steph said as she led them there.

"Here we are," she said.

"This is niceee," Tyson said as he looked around in awe. He thought his house was nice, but Steph's was beautiful and felt home-y.

"Yeah I like all the pillows," Diana said.

"Thanks guys. So, we can do everything here. There's an outlet in case your laptops die, there's a blank sheet over there to protect the floor against the paint, and a projector over there so we can all look at the PowerPoint better," Steph explained.

"Wow, you think of everything huh?" Diana asked.

"I try," Steph said with a chuckle.

"We should be all set then…I call the bean bag!" Tyson said as he jumped on it before anyone could challenge his request.

"Aww I wanted that onee…okay I'll take the couch," Diana said.

"I'll take the floor!" Steph said as she plopped onto the ground.

"…. And yes, I know that that is literally the only place I could go, but I just wanted to join in the fun," Steph said with a chuckle.

"HaHa. You can be excited about the floor if you want to, we won't judge you, no need to explain," Tyson said with a grin.

"Okay let's get started then," Steph said with a bright smile.

It only took a few minutes before the room got silent. They all worked intently on their work and before they knew it an hour had passed and Steph's Dad came with the long-awaited finger sandwiches.

Diana took one bite and she said, "Oh...oh wow...This is good, like good good. What's in this?!"

"He won't tell me. He said it's a secret and he'd tell me when I get older," Steph said, rolling her eyes.

"You have to try some Tyson!" Diana said with her mouth stuffed.

"I am, I am... I just want to get to a stopping point. I don't want to lose my thought," Tyson replied, still typing away on his laptop.

"All I have to say is don't be mad if there's none left for you," Diana replied with a smirk.

"Ha. I know Steph will save me one," Tyson said with a smirk.

"You know I got you," Steph said while giving him an exploding fist bump.

"You're supposed to have my side...shame...shame," Diana said with a chuckle.

"Hey, what can I say? I really want him to try at least one so I can see his reaction to how good it tastes," Steph said.

"And here I thought you just cared about my wellbeing and need for food to give me energy for my work...shame," Tyson said with a chuckle.

"Dang, why are you all ganging up on me now? This is my house, remember. And you guys are just shaming me," Steph reminded them.

"Oh yes, I'm sorryyyyy," Tyson said right before him and Diana started busting out laughing.

"Haha, very funny...And you must have reached a stopping point since you can talk so much," Steph said.

"As a matter of fact, I am and I'm going to try one now...Oh wowww," He said as he stuffed his mouth.

"It's good isn't it?" Steph asked.

"Uhhuh...This is really good," Tyson said with his eyes closed, savoring the explosion of deliciousness happening in his mouth.

"And I rest my case," Steph said as she leaned back against the couch.

Within ten minutes, all the finger sandwiches were gone. They were about to start back working but then Steph hit Tyson with a paper ball that she said was by accident. It started a paper ball war that lasted about twenty minutes full of laughter and screaming. They got so loud Steph's Dad came from upstairs wondering if they were okay and they had to calm down. They took it as a sign that they should start back working again. In about an hour and a half, Diana and Steph heard light snoring and they looked at each other and laughed. They know he was notorious for napping after he finished his work, they swore he must not get a lot of sleep at night.

"Are you done yet, Diana?" Steph asked

"I have one slide left before the end slide, what about you?" Diana asked.

"I have to wait till this part dries and I can add the final touches," Steph said while looking at her masterpiece. She could see the A+ in her future.

"That sounds good," Diana said.

When Diana had finished her PowerPoint, she considered waking Tyson up but decided to leave him alone. "Maybe that's why he was like that in the car. He must have been tired," Diana thought to herself. When she looked at Steph's work, she was in awe. She knew Steph was talented but she really had a gift. It looked so life-like, she even textured the plants. Steph was so focused she didn't even notice Diana was staring.

"Steph, that looks amazing! Do you plan on becoming an artist?" Diana asked.

"Me?! No, but thank you," Steph said.

"Why not? You definitely have the talent. You could be the next Frida Kahlo or something," Diana exclaimed.

"Wow...you really think so?!" Steph said.

"Duh, that's why I said it. So, what's stopping you from doing it as a career? Do you love it?" Diana asked

"Yes, I do."

"Okay, do you think you're good at it?"

"Yes, I would like to think so," Steph said.

"Then what's holding you back?" Diana asked.

"It's just that the world can be really judgmental and it's hard to tell what constructive criticism I should actually pay attention to or ignore, because it's usually just people being mean. And before you say I shouldn't care what people think, that's literally what is going to make or break my career, whether people actually *like* my art. So, their opinion does matter. I just don't know if I could handle that."

"I don't want you to think of it that way. You're talented and a great person. What is there not to like about you? You cannot convince me that out of seven-point-eight billion people that live on this planet that no one will like your art," Diana said.

"I guess that's true. It *is* very unlikely," Steph said.

"So that part about your career depending on people liking your work isn't something you should worry about. As long as you keep pushing yourself, learning new techniques, and keep producing quality work like that, then you will be just fine. I believe in you and you should too," Diana said as she nudged her shoulder.

"That's so sweet...Don't make me cry," Steph said.

"No crying! I mean it and about those haters...they are irrelevant. Someone will always have something to say about whatever you do whether it's about your art or just anything in general. You can't worry about that, you might as well do what makes you happy," Diana said.

"Okay...that's not making me feel any better and plus as an artist you have to listen to criticism. It's what shows that you are mature and willing to work on yourself and your art; as well as letting people know that you aren't cocky and know that everything can be improved."

"But not all criticism is constructive. I agree that accepting criticism is important in that field, but you have to learn the difference and act accordingly. A simple "I don't like that. It looks terrible" is not constructive criticism and doesn't provide any means for you to change your work in any way. Constructive criticism is all about actually helping construct something, build something up. So, if a statement doesn't offer something for you to build onto then it isn't worth your energy or time," Diana explained.

"Okay, but constructive criticism can be harsh sometimes," Steph said.

"It can be, but the only part you should focus on is the constructive part of the comment and honestly you don't actually *have* to take the constructive criticism either. You can do whatever you want with your work. You can politely accept their criticism without actually doing what they say. If you truly think what they suggested will elevate your work, then use it and if you don't like it then don't. You and your view of your work doesn't have to change for anyone. No one else's opinions truly matter," Diana said.

"I get that, but that doesn't mean the words still won't hurt. *You* understand that better than anyone," Steph said.

"Well, yes they do but you can do affirmations to heal yourself from the hurt so that way it won't stick with you, and you'll have me and Tyson by your side the whole way," Diana said.

"Even knowing that doesn't really make me feel better cause it still means I'll get hurt. I'm not like you, Diana. You get upset when people talk about you, I get sad," Steph said.

"I wouldn't say getting upset is any better," Diana said.

"But all you have to do is calm down and you'll be fine. I would probably be crying every time," Steph said.

"Getting all worked up every time and not knowing how to release all that anger isn't better than crying," Diana assured her.

"Well, I don't know how to deal with it then," Steph said while putting her face in her hands. Just talking about it made her feel overwhelmed.

"I don't have all the answers but I certainly don't think you should let that stop you from doing something you love, especially when you're that good at it. Plus, we have all the time in the world to think about careers," Diana said.

"I'll think about it," Steph said.

How about we leave Tyson down here since he decided to take a nap and ask your Dad if he has any more finger sandwiches and maybe you can talk to Mr. Vendetta tomorrow. He can help you," Diana suggested.

"Okay. And I almost forgot Tyson was here..." Steph said.

"No, you didn't," Diana said with an eye roll and smirk as she got up.

"Yeah I didn't," Steph said and they shared a laugh.

"Let's go then!" Diana yelled softly, careful not to wake Tyson.

"Nice try... I'm going to get more too," Tyson said as he got up from the bean bag with a yawn.

"Did you umm...happen to hear everything we talked about," Steph said nervously.

"You'll never know...Race you guys there!" Tyson said as he started running to the kitchen with a smile.

"No fair, you got a head start!" Diana yelled as she ran after him with Steph close behind.

Luckily, there were a good bit of finger sandwiches left that made Steph smile. It was getting late and Diana's Mom was on her way to Steph's house to pick up Diana and Tyson. So, after they ate the rest of the sandwiches they packed up their stuff and waited in the foyer for Diana's Mom. They were sitting there for a while waiting on Ms. Monroe.

"Soo…umm, can your Mom take me home?" Tyson asked Diana.

"Yes, my Mom already told me she'll take you home," Diana said.

"Okay great," Tyson said, releasing all the tension he didn't even know he was holding.

"You have to do better, you could have asked that earlier," Diana said.

"I know I know," Tyson said with a shake of his head.

"Yeah, parents don't like last-minute things and you know we would've taken you home. I asked you over," Steph said.

"I know, your Dad is just kind of intimidating," Tyson said.

"My Dad? Really?" Steph asked.

"Yes, your Dad…" Tyson said.

"Haha…I don't see that," Diana said.

"Me neither. My Dad is super nice," Steph said.

"My feelings are not for you all to understand," Tyson said.

"Touché," Diana and Steph said in unison.

The doorbell rang and it was Ms. Monroe.

"Hey guys, how did the project come along?" she asked.

"It turned out really nice," Diana said with a thumbs up while grabbing all her stuff.

"That's great, tell your Dad I said thank you for letting Diana come over," Ms. Monroe said to Steph.

"I will. Bye guys!" Steph said as she waved to Tyson and Diana.

"Bye see you tomorrow," Diana said.

"Bye see ya," Tyson said.

They all walked to the car...

"So, do you know how to get to your house from here? Do we need to go back and print out some directions?" Ms. Monroe asked.

"Oh no I printed out directions at home. I had asked Steph what her address was yesterday," Tyson replied.

"How can you be so well prepared and not at the exact same time?" Diana asked while tilting her head.

"I don't know, my uncle says I've always been like that," Tyson said.

"Okay well let's go, hand them here. Is it far?" Ms. Monroe asked.

"No, it isn't too far from here," Tyson replied as he handed the directions to her and got in the car.

"Okay," Ms. Monroe said.

The car ride felt long to Diana, but it turned out to be about 15 minutes, so not that bad. Tyson wasn't talking again. "He could just have nothing to say," Diana thought. However, something just didn't feel right to her. She decided not to ask him about it. "He might have just had a bad morning or no sleep. He did fall asleep again at Steph's house for a good while, so it's possible," Diana thought. When they reached his driveway, they were greeted with a black gateway and could only see a glimpse of the house that they knew had to be huge. Tyson gave Ms. Monroe the key code and when they drove a bit more they saw his very modern glass-walled house and Diana's mouth was wide open.

"You live here?!" Diana asked excitedly.

"Yeah, maybe one day you and Steph can come over sometime. You guys would be the first people to come over to my house," Tyson said.

"That would be great!" Diana said.

"And an adult would be there, too right?" Ms. Monroe asked.

"Of course. My uncle would be there," Tyson replied.

"Okay, well you go ahead and get inside and we will wait until you go in and close the door before we drive off, okay?" **Ms. Monroe said.**

"Alright. Bye, and thank you for the ride!" Tyson said right before he ran inside and closed the door.

As Diana and her Mom pulled off they both looked at each other in awe.

"That was a nice house," Diana said.

"Yeah, it's very big. You did say his parents were doctors soo… "Ms. Monroe said.

"Yeah, but I like our house though and I'm ready to get back to it and sleep off those finger sandwiches," Diana said.

"I like our house too and you all had finger sandwiches?" Ms. Monroe asked.

"Yes, oh my goodness you have to try it one day. You will eat at least five and probably more after you have a break. Steph's Dad's secret sauce is ingenious. I don't know what's in it, but I could eat it like soup," Diana ranted.

"Okay, okay but it's not better than my famous lasagna, right?" Ms. Monroe asked with a raised eyebrow.

"Pshh, of course not. Nothing can beat your lasagna," Diana said with a smile.

"That's right," Ms. Monroe said as she gave Diana a high-five with a big smile.

When Tyson got in the house, he felt a sense of relief. He had been constantly thinking about how he was betraying his friends by not telling them about Mr. Vendetta. He wanted to keep his promise but it's been a week and he *still* hasn't told Diana yet. "I'm going to talk to him tomorrow, I have to. I can't just keep holding this in. I can barely sleep. I barely made it through class. Diana and Steph are my first real friends, I can't let them down. Mr. Vendetta has to tell Diana soon," Tyson thought to himself.

It was the next morning and Tyson made it a point to wake up extra early to walk to school to be able to talk with Mr. Vendetta without Diana and Steph questioning it. He was so early; the assistant principal's car wasn't in his usual parking space and he was always there on time. He felt relieved when the entrance double doors were actually open, he didn't plan out what he would have done if they had been locked. He was hoping that Mr. Vendetta was in his office. "If the door was open then he should be in there," Tyson thought.

He turned out to be correct, when he got to his office door, it was cracked open and Mr. Vendetta was sitting in his spinning chair.

"You're here pretty early. Is everything okay, Tyson?" Mr. Vendetta asked.

"No, it's not. I can't take this anymore. You have to tell her…" Tyson pleaded.

"Oh, you mean about my powers…" Mr. Vendetta said with a sigh.

"Yes, the ones that are the same as Diana's that you haven't told her about, that I'm withholding from my closest friends," Tyson said as he closed the door to keep anyone from overhearing.

"I will tell her soon, just give me some time," Mr. Vendetta said.

"With all due respect sir, I can't. I'm barely getting any sleep. Luckily, they know I like taking naps so they aren't too suspicious, but I can't keep hiding this from them. They are my friends. I know that may not seem like much to you but it means everything to me. I haven't had many people in my life really care about me and want to hang out with me and include me in things. I'm usually alone and while I don't mind it, I still really enjoy my newfound company with my friends. I don't want this to be the reason they kick me to the curb. I need you to tell them or I will. I can't wait any longer...sir," Tyson said.

"Okay, I will tell her later today," Mr. Vendetta said. He could tell how much this weighed on Tyson. He never meant to burden him so much and knew he had to make it right, somehow.

"Thank you, sir," Tyson said as he walked out the door.

"Ohhh, hey Steph, you're here early," Tyson said nervously.

"Yeah, I need to ask Yoda about something. Why are you here, did you need to talk to him too?" Steph asked.

"Yeah, I had to talk to him about something…Uhh, nothing major," Tyson said with an unusual smile.

"Uh-huh… Alright well I'll see you later," Steph said.

"See you later," Tyson said as he speed-walked away.

"I wonder why he's acting like that. He has been acting weird lately… something definitely is up. Maybe he had to talk to Mr. Vendetta about some personal problems too…Yeah that's probably it. It must be hard being alone like that all the time while your parents are at work. Hopefully, he'll open up to me at some point," Steph thought to herself. She then shoved that thought aside as she opened Mr. Vendetta's door.

"Hey, Yoda," Steph said.

"Yoda?" Mr. Vendetta asked.

"Yes, it has a nice ring to it, don't you think? It's because you give good, sometimes confusing advice...I need to know if you can help me with something," Steph asked.

"Sure, I'll help you. What is going on?" Mr. Vendetta asked.

"I know words hurt and I want to be an artist, but I don't think I can handle the harsh critiques. I was hoping you could help me deal with it. I know I'm not supposed to care what other people think-"

"But it still bothers you right? "Mr. Vendetta chimed in.

"Yes, and Diana told me about how I can heal myself but I don't want to cry every time I see a hateful comment or harsh criticism. I can't be like that if I want art to be my career," Steph continued.

"Okay, so what I suggest is taking a sheet of paper, write the comment that hurt you down on the piece of paper, and throw it away in the trash." Mr. Vendetta instructed.

"I don't understand. How would that help me?" Steph asked.

"Writing the comment down takes it out of your head, turning it from a mental thing to a physical thing. Then, once it has become tangible, you can rip it up, showing the insignificance of the comment, and throw it away, putting that comment in the trash where it belongs."

"Okay, I get it now, but I don't want the words to hurt so bad that it makes me cry. And Diana told me about the defensive affirmations, but I feel like that works best when you are actually going back and forth with someone," Steph explained.

"I suggest regular everyday affirmations. See, what allows a person to be mostly unbothered by other people's words is their strong belief in themselves and how they view themselves and their work. It's like someone telling you your stupid for thinking two plus two equals four on a test you were about to turn it. How would that make you feel?"

"I wouldn't care because I know I'm right and that I will get the answer right when the test gets handed back."

"Yes, exactly. When you master that same undoubting attitude toward yourself and your art then the words will not affect you the same. However, it does intrigue me that you added in that when you got the test back it would be marked correct, leading me to believe that you, in fact, seek external validation. You want to feel reassured by others," Mr. Vendetta said.

"Yes, it's very comforting to be told people like my work. Is that bad?"

"No, that's that bad. But needing to be told that is. That is very dangerous, especially in your field. If someone was to tell you that they thought your artwork sucked, would that hurt your feelings?" Mr. Vendetta asked.

"It would," Steph replied.

"There's nothing wrong with finding comfort in other people liking your art. But giving other people power over how you feel is not the best for you. I say giving them power because you only feel that way because you allowed their comment to hurt you. It doesn't have to affect you in that way. Yes, words are powerful, but you have the power to change how the words affect you, it doesn't have to hurt you. You can shift it into fuel to use as motivation to keep pressing on. Do you often ask for feedback?"

"Yes, I usually ask people how they like it," Steph replied.

"I suggest you stop asking people how they like your work if you aren't fully prepared *yet* for their reply. Do your affirmations every morning until you start to truly believe what you're saying and then focus on after hearing negative comments shifting them into fuel instead of letting it fuel your tears."

"Okay, do you know any affirmations I could use? I'm new to the whole affirmations thing," Steph asked.

"You want to be an artist, right?" Mr. Vendetta asked.

"Yes, I do," Steph replied with confidence. Mr. Vendetta smiled.

"You can say: My hard work will show in my work. My work is a reflection of me and is, therefore beautiful, as am I. My work is amazing as it is. I am brilliant. I am strong and my work will make a difference," Mr. Vendetta said.

"Thank you so much, Yoda," Steph said.

"Those are only a few but you know yourself better than anyone and you know what you need to hear the most. So, whatever that is, repeat it to yourself every day, consistently, until you feel like you are ready to start asking people how your work is and can handle whatever their response will be," Mr. Vendetta insisted.

"I definitely will. Thanks, I knew I could count on you," Steph said as she walked out the door. He gave her *a lot* to think about and the day barely started, but she was grateful for everything he had to say.

By the time Steph was finished talking to Mr. Vendetta, she had to practically run to class to make it on time. When she arrived, she saw Diana and Tyson in their usual seats and she sat in hers as well, ready to present her artwork to the class.

"Good Morning, class," Mr. Campbell said.

"Good morning," the class groggily replied.

"As you all know, today is the day for everyone to present their projects. Who would like to go first?" Mr. Campbell asked.

"We will," Steph said confidently while raising her hand.

"Okay! I love the enthusiasm. Stephanie's group come right up and present your project to the class," Mr. Campbell instructed.

Diana, a little shocked that Steph wanted to actually go first after their conversation last night, went ahead and brought the flash drive to Mr. Campbell so he could display the PowerPoint on the screen. Since Tyson was in charge of the paper, essentially all he had to do was turn it in and sit down, but he decided to stand next to Steph and Diana as they presented their work. Steph unveiled her project, covered by the plastic bag and the class' eyes lit up in awe of her painting. Steph started to explain the scenery depicted in her work to the class and Tyson could tell no one was really listening to what she was saying, only staring at her work, and Tyson couldn't help but do the same. Mr. Campbell even toned out for a second, because once she was done presenting, it took for Diana to do a fake cough to get his attention to start the PowerPoint. Diana then started going over the PowerPoint she made and at the end, the class clapped hysterically. Then, they went back to their seats and Mr. Campbell asked the next group to come up and present their project.

This went on for the whole class until every group was done presenting, continuing even after they had gone to lunch. Since Mr. Campbell knew by the end of all those presentations that the students were worn out, he let them talk for the rest of class time. By the time Mr. Campbell announced he would let the class talk for the rest of class and sat back at his desk, Tyson was already asleep and snoring, or so Diana and Steph thought.

"Is it just me or is Tyson sleeping a lot more lately?" Diana asked Steph.

"Oh no," Tyson said to himself as he fake snored.

"No, I've noticed it too. I think him being alone all the time is weighing on him. I saw him leaving Mr.

Vendetta's office this morning. He was probably looking for some advice," Steph said.

"Well that's not exactly the case," Tyson thought to himself.

"I guess you could be right...but he's been fine up until recently. I don't know what has changed. He said he's been used to being by himself for years. What makes this year different?" Diana said.

"Maybe we should try and get together more often to make him feel less lonely," Steph said.

"No, anything but that...I can't keep lying to you all. Hopefully, Mr. Vendetta will keep up his end of the deal by the end of today...I just can't take the lying by omission to my friends," Tyson thought to himself.

"Yeah, I think he would like that. I've been really busy studying and practicing my debate speech for the mock debate. So, I'll be more available after," Diana explained.

"Great, that gives Mr. Vendetta time to tell her before they ask me to hang out," Tyson thought, feeling relieved.

"Oh yeah, I forgot about that. Are you excited?" Steph asked.

"Yeah, I'm excited. Just a bit stressed. I really want to make it to the real competition," Diana replied.

"Don't stress yourself out worrying about what might happen and focus like you've been doing and build the best argument you can for the sharks and let your hard work speak for itself."

"I guess you're right. I don't have much time left, though," Diana said.

"Yea, I know. Tyson and I will be there cheering you on," Steph said.

"Wellllll, I don't know if people are actually allowed to come...but come anyway please," Diana said.

"Even if we have to sneak in just to see you we will. We have your back," Steph said.

Hearing that really hit Tyson hard. It made him that more excited about Mr. Vendetta telling Diana everything later that day so he could stop hiding it from them. The bell finally rang for dismissal and Tyson pretended like he was waking up and looked around and was starting to get worried because Mr. Vendetta hadn't come in and asked to speak to Diana. "Well, I guess it would be weird for the janitor to come in and ask for a student," Tyson thought to himself. Then just as everyone started getting up he caught a glimpse of Mr. Vendetta near the door and he was able to breathe again.

"Glad to see you finally awake," Steph said.

"Oh yeah, I've just been tired lately," Tyson said.

"We could tell, see you all tomorrow," Steph said as she gave Diana and Tyson a hug goodbye.

"Bye, Tyson," Diana waved as she proceeded to walk out the door.

"Bye, Diana," Tyson said, hoping after he tells her she won't be upset with him.

As Diana walks out the door, she is stopped by Mr. Vendetta. He then asks her to come with him to his office because he has something to tell her. Diana is a little concerned but follows him anyway.

"What's going on Mr. Vendetta?" Diana asked.

"Well, I wanted to talk to you about Tyson," Mr. Vendetta said.

"Oh, umm okay," Diana said.

"Have you noticed anything off about him lately?" Mr. Vendetta said.

"Well, he has been extra sleepy lately and his snoring is getting a bit louder than normal, but other than that, that's it," Diana replies.

"You see, he has sleep apnea. That is why he is always sleepy, and it's been difficult for him to handle it lately, because he didn't know how to tell you and Stephanie. He's been beating himself up about it because he's been feeling like he has been lying to you two," Mr. Vendetta said.

"Ohh, woww, what exactly is sleep apnea?" Diana asked.

"It's a sleeping disorder, you don't have to concern yourself with the specifics, but basically it makes him sleepy, snore, and it gets worse if he doesn't try and get sleep at home. He had come to me this morning telling me how he couldn't bring himself to sleep at night because he's been lying to you and Steph about his disorder and how he wanted me to tell you for him," Mr. Vendetta said.

"I don't know why he just didn't tell us," Diana said.

"Don't be upset with him. Having a disorder is seen as a weakness and you guys are his first real friends and he doesn't want to lose you all if you all thought he was weird," Mr. Vendetta explains.

"I have powers and he thinks that I would stop being friends with him because he has a disorder...I would never and neither would Steph," Diana said.

"I know that. However, he was scared. Not everyone is nice and accepting as you would hope in this world. You guys are his first real friends and he wanted to seem perfect to you all so you would stay, it's not crazy reasoning when you haven't experienced true friendship before like you all have now," Mr. Vendetta explained.

"Well, thanks for telling me and I will tell Steph tomorrow," Diana said.

"Before you go, I know he asked me to tell you. However, he doesn't like talking about it. Just tell him it's no big deal and that it doesn't change anything. The best thing you can do is keep your all's normal routine and don't bring it up," Mr. Vendetta strongly encourages.

"Okay, will do and I'll tell Steph to do the same," Diana says as she heads out the door.

"Have a good day," Mr. Vendetta said.

"You too," Diana said right before the door shut.

When the door shut, Mr. Vendetta felt a great sense of relief. His story was tight and hopefully, Diana will do as he said and not bring it up. "At least that will keep Tyson off my back. Diana doesn't need to know about me yet."

That night Diana talked to her Mom about it, because she knew Mr. Vendetta told her not to talk about it, but it just didn't sit right with her. Ms. Monroe came up with the same conclusion Mr. Vendetta did; that she shouldn't bring it up. She said "by you and Steph not mentioning it and doing things as you usually do, you are actually implying that you don't think he is weird and that it doesn't change anything about your friendship; especially if this is something he doesn't really feel comfortable talking about. When people get in uncomfortable situations they push people away. So, you don't want to keep bringing it up if it makes him uncomfortable and it ends up pushing him away." When Ms. Monroe put it that way, Diana could see why that would be the best option. It's just the truth is she did care about his disorder, not in a way that made him seem weird, but she wanted him to know that he could talk to him about anything, she wanted him to feel comfortable enough to tell her. She hoped their bond was strong enough, but she remembered what her Mom had told her when she was younger, "You can't force others to feel the same way you do, just like you can't force others to do what you want. Well, I guess she was wrong about the last part…Hopefully, Steph won't be hurt he didn't tell her," Diana thought to herself.

The next morning, Diana woke up and from then until she walked through Pedita's double doors, she rehearsed what she would say to Steph. "So, Tyson has sleep apnea, which is why he is always so tired. He was afraid to tell us because he didn't want us to not be his friends anymore. But both Mr. Vendetta and my Mom said that we shouldn't really bring it up and just pretend like everything is just as it was…yeah that'll work…I hope," Diana thinks to herself.

When Diana walked in she saw Steph in her usual spot by the door and luckily Tyson wasn't there yet. Diana walked over to Steph and told her she needed to talk to her by the restroom.

"Hey, what are we talking about?" Steph asked.

"Well…it's about Tyson," Diana replied.

"I knew something was going on. I felt it. What did he say?" Steph said.

"You remember when you saw him leaving Mr. Vendetta's office and suspected something was bothering him? Well it turns out he has sleep apnea and he asked Mr. Vendetta if he could tell us for him because he was scared we would look at him differently and not want to be friends with him anymore," Diana said.

"I guess I could understand why he wouldn't want to tell us. That is something really personal, but we would never judge him for it. I thought he knew that. I mean...We're friends," Steph said with her head laying low.

"I know. I told Mr. Vendetta that it was crazy for him to think we'd leave," Diana said.

"You even have superpowers yet we stayed with you, haha," Steph said.

"I know right. The weird one of the bunch is me," Diana said.

"And we wouldn't have it any other way," Steph said.

"Oh, but both my Mom and Mr. Vendetta said to not talk to him about it," Diana said.

"What? Why not?" Steph asked.

"They said it would be better if we didn't bring it up and act like nothing's changed and just go about our regular schedule," Diana said.

"I mean...nothing has changed. It's just I want him to know that his having sleep apnea doesn't mean I care about him any less or just change the way I feel about him in general. I want him to know he can come to us about anything," Steph said.

"Well, my Mom put it this way; because we are his first group of real friends he isn't really familiar with how accepting we are to each other and maybe acting like nothing has changed will give him the reassurance that he could tell us stuff in the future and that we won't judge him," Diana said.

"I guess that's one way of thinking about it...Okay I won't talk about it then," Steph said.

"Great because I sort of told Mr. Vendetta we wouldn't already," Diana said.

"Okay, well we have to get to class now before we are late," Steph said.

On the way to the classroom, Diana could tell that Steph wasn't very happy about the situation and truthfully, she wasn't either, but she didn't want to push Tyson away. When they walked inside and saw Tyson they both tried to be as normal as possible, just giving him a glance and a hey.

Tyson noticed something was off and he immediately drew the conclusion that Diana and Steph were mad at him for not telling him. During class, Steph didn't raise her hand once to give the answer to a problem and it made Tyson really worry. He knew he needed to talk to her about it. Then, he thought that he should probably apologize to Diana first since it affected her the most. "But it would probably be weird if I talked to them separately...I'll just talk to them at lunch," Tyson thought to himself.

When it was time to go to lunch Diana, Steph, and Tyson all walked together. However, it seemed more like they were walking individually in the same direction, barely looking at one another. When they reached the table with their trays, they started to eat or at least play with their food (Steph). He knew he needed to be the one to bring it up.

"Sooo, I take it that Mr. Vendetta told y'all?" Tyson asked.

"Yeah, HE did," Steph said.

"I'm sorry for not telling you sooner," Tyson said.

"Why, didn't you tell us? Do you not trust us?" Steph asked.

"I do trust you. I just didn't want y'all to not want to be friends with me anymore since I lied to you all for so long," Tyson explained.

"We are your friends, you can tell us anything," Steph said.

"I know…I know…And I promise I will from now on," Tyson said.

"Well Diana, how do you feel about hi-"

"It doesn't change anything," Diana said while interrupting him.

"Really?" Tyson asked.

"Really, it isn't a big deal," Diana replied.

"Yeah, it really isn't," Steph said.

"Oh, okay then...Now, can I see the two of you smile and get a hug please?" Tyson asked.

"Of course," Steph said as she and Diana gave Tyson a hug.

When they got back to class, Steph and Diana were raising their hands to participate in class discussions while Tyson was fighting off sleep, eventually losing the battle toward the end of the class causing the girls to chuckle as they looked at him now with new understanding. Meanwhile, Mr. Vendetta had come to the conclusion that Diana didn't bring it up because she hadn't barged in looking for answers. He knew he would tell her one day, "Just not right now," he told himself as he was walking to the faculty meeting.

CHAPTER 4:

REALIZATION

It was the day before the mock debate competition and Diana was trying not to stress, but it was to no avail. Ms. Monroe noticed Diana had been in her room almost all day and figured she was cramming for her debate. So, she fixed some chamomile tea to help with studying and relaxing. When she brought it up to her room, she found Diana glued to the computer screen and she forced her to take a break and drink some tea as well as reminding her she has to get some sleep or she won't remember what she researched. Even though Mr. Kyle said he would allow them to have notecards, Diana wanted to be fully prepared and not have to reference her notecards at all. When it was time to bed she went to sleep hopeful she would win and

Realization

get a chance to prove Hannah wrong and stay in control of her powers.

The next morning Diana was awoken by the aroma of her Mom's famous grand-slam breakfast she made for very special occasions. Diana jumped out of bed and almost fell downstairs trying to get to the kitchen. When Diana reached the end of the stairs, Ms. Monroe asked

"How was your sleep? Are you ready for your special breakfast?"

"It was fine, but more importantly…I'm excited about my breakfast!" Diana exclaimed as she plopped down in her seat at the table.

"I was hoping it would mentally put you on the right track today. I cooked all your favorites: waffles, omelets, muffins, bacon, and sausage."

"Thank you so much, Mommy!" Diana said.

"Your welcome, baby. Go ahead and eat so you can get ready for your big day! I know you will do well, it's written in your genes like your Momma," Ms. Monroe said with a smirk.

"You never did debate in school Mom, haha," Diana said while starting to eat.

"I'll have you know that I may never have formerly been on the debate team, but I have won a lot and I do mean a lot of arguments in my day," Ms. Monroe retorted.

"Debating isn't technically arguing though, Mom," Diana said.

"Oh, debating is, arguing with researched facts in front of a crowd haha…yes, baby, they are soooo different…hahaha," Ms. Monroe said.

"Haha, I guess you're right," Diana said.

"Either way, I know that you're just like your Momma and you will knock this out the park," Ms. Monroe said.

"Thanks Mom," Diana said.

"Okay now, hurry up so you can get to school on time. I'll be there to pick you up at 5:00 pm, right after y'all are done, and I want to hear about it as soon as you get in the car!" Mr. Monroe said.

"I sure will!" Diana said, eating the last bit of her breakfast in practically three bites.

After Diana got ready, she raced to the car. The drive to school felt like forever, but she was able to catch the glimpse of a yellow butterfly, like the ones that light up in her room and she knew it was going to be a good day. When she arrived at the school, her Mom initiated their good-luck hand gesture where they would lock pinkies and kiss the side of their thumb. Then Diana got out of the car and went through the double doors feeling confident and ready for her competition today; she had done all she could to prepare herself and today her hard work paid off. Once she stepped through the doors Steph and Tyson were there with a poster board that read, "Go Diana!!! You got this!" on it and some starbursts.

"Aww thank you guys so much," Diana said

"We are going to hold it up when it's your turn when we watch you debate!" Steph said.

"Me and Steph planned this a while ago. We thought we should surprise you with something to show you how much we believe in you," Tyson said.

"You guys are the best friends ever!" Diana said as she pulled them into a tight hug.

They started having a casual conversation and then Diana felt a tap on her shoulder, it was Mr. Vendetta.

"Hey, Mr. vendetta. Today's the day of the mock trial competition," Diana said.

"I know, I've been keeping tabs on everything. I'm very excited for you. Just remember why I wanted you to join the debate team originally, you are in control of yourself and your power, you will make everyone proud," Mr. Vendetta said.

"I know and I'm ready," Diana said.

"Okay well, you better go inside. The bell is about to ring", Mr. Vendetta said.

"Okay, Yoda," Steph replied as she and Diana walked into the classroom, making Mr. Vendetta chuckle.

"Wait Mr. Vendetta. I just want to say thank you for telling them. I was actually able to get some sleep last night, I really appreciate you keeping your promise. Okay, I have to go. Bye, Mr. Vendetta," Tyson said as he ran to class.

"Bye, Tyson," Mr. Vendetta said. He knew that the lie wouldn't hold forever, but at least it could give Tyson some comfort while I figure out what to say.

At the end of class, Diana was focused on her note cards, re-reading them to make sure she knew all her points. As she researched more and more she became a fan of sharks and saw herself, by doing this debate, a shark protection activist. She would be on stage facing Hannah in exactly thirty more minutes. The thought of Steph and Tyson being there made her heart fill with warmth. She started to think about how she thought the debate would go.

Realization

"Who am I going to debate with? I really hope it isn't Hannah. Would that really mean I wouldn't make it to the main competition? Am I going to be able to hit all my points in under eight minutes?" Diana was thinking to herself which only ceased once the bell rang, signaling that it was time for her to head to the auditorium for the debate.

"Okay, Diana. We are going ahead to get there to find a good seat. You got this!" Steph said and she and Tyson ran to the auditorium.

When Steph and Tyson entered the auditorium, they found no other student in the room.

"I guess this isn't something people normally come to, oh well, more opportunity for Diana to be able to see us cheer her on," Steph said

"Yeah, at least we can sit right in the front," Tyson said.

"Umm, I don't think we should sit directly in the front. It might be a little intimidating. Let's sit front-side. Yeah, that's better," Steph said.

"Okay, lead the way," Tyson said while gesturing to the seats.

Meanwhile, Diana is backstage in the auditorium waiting to hear the list of competitors. Mr. Kyle was a little more dressed up today than he has been in the past and he stood tall as he announced the list. Diana closed her eyes and crossed her fingers as she waited to hear her name. She was just about to open her eyes and he said "Diana Monroe vs. Hannah McCafee" and Diana's mouth dropped. However, she quickly gathered herself and got her head in the game. Then once she was back focused she saw Hannah approaching her.

"Are you ready to fail?" Hannah asked.

"I'm thoroughly prepared and ready to do my best," Diana replied.

"Aww that's what all losers say," Hannah said.

"You say that until you see how awesome my best is," Diana said as she walked to her side of the stage.

"Whatever..." Hannah said as she proceeded to walk in the opposite direction.

"Okay girls. I'm going to tell you both how the mock debate will proceed. First, Diana, you will be presenting your affirmative resolution. Then, Hannah, you will be presenting your opposing resolution. Afterward, you two will go again as a last resort to persuade me on your viewpoint, countering your opponent's argument. Since this is a mock debate that I am using to decide who I want on the competition team, there will be no winner. Do your best and impress me. Are you two ready?" Mr. Kyle asked.

"Yes," they said in unison.

"Okay, let's begin. Diana, you're up," Mr. Kyle said.

An excerpt from Diana's speech:

How would you feel if while walking to the grocery store something grabs you and tears off your arm leaving you to bleed out? Not only you, but your friends and family as well? That is what is happening to sharks. They are getting captured specifically for their fins. It is called Finning. Their fins are considered delicacies in certain countries. So, fishermen have made shark finning their main priority. Yes, shark fins can be eaten but the question is should they? Should fishermen be allowed to capture sharks, de-fin them and throw them back into the ocean to die? Just because we can, doesn't always mean we should. Sharks are vital to our ecosystem. They make sure the fish that eat on our precious reefs stay within a range that allows for the reefs to continue to flourish. Those are the same reefs that account for half of the world's oxygen, that we breathe every day, and absorb nearly one-third of the carbon dioxide that is produced by the burning of fossil fuels. If 11.5 thousand sharks continue to get slaughtered every hour. We will end up wiping out an entire species of precious creatures that would lead to less oxygen for us to breathe and less absorbed carbon dioxide in our air....

"Okay, thank you, Diana. Hannah, it is your turn," Mr. Kyle instructed.

An excerpt from Hannah's speech:

How would you feel if you were on vacation with your family only to be brutally attacked by a shark while surfing causing your life to forever be changed? Finning may be unfortunate for the sharks, but it would save around ten people each year that die by the hand of sharks. Ten people may not seem like a lot of people but in just five years, that number of people who have died turns to fifty, in six years it's 60, in 10 years it's 100 deaths; should I continue? Shark finning is more like controlling the shark population. It has even been banned in several countries to make sure the number of sharks that die doesn't exceed a certain amount. Also, who are we to determine what people should be allowed to eat? That would be a violation of human rights, specifically the right to food when the food does not pose harm to humans. Humans are our brothers and sisters. Whereas sharks are just vicious animals that kill us. I would argue sharks don't deserve to be protected as much as they are being right now...

At this point, Diana is trying to calm herself down. While spending hours researching sharks, their tendencies/behavior, and their role in the environment. Diana had grown fond of them and realized that they have been misunderstood and not at all how they are portrayed in the movies. So, listening to Hannah belittle them and call them vicious when they are the opposite, shy, not aggressive and bad hunters. They are getting annihilated by humans and it's not fair, "all for a tough, almost tasteless dish," Diana thought to herself.

Meanwhile, Steph and Tyson had been watching from the side.

"Diana did really good, but I'm not going to lie...Hannah was also very convincing," Steph said.

"I agree, it is difficult to argue with the death of humans," Tyson said.

"I've actually watched a documentary on sharks and they are not at all how Hannah described them. Diana is probably really upset, having to listen to her talk down on them like that."

"I haven't done actual research, but I've always thought that the movies exaggerated things, with the whole 'one drop of blood will cause a shark to come from miles away just to eat you.' I find it ridiculous to be honest," Tyson said.

"I'm happy I'm not the only one," Steph replied.

"But, we should really watch Diana, we don't want her to use her power in front of them. She can't get too upset," Steph said.

"But what exactly can we do? We can't just interrupt the debate," Tyson.

"We can make something up. We can say we have an emergency...Yea, no that won't work. I'll just distract her if I sense it about to happen," Steph said confidently with her head held high.

"And how do you plan on doing that, exactly?" Tyson asked with a slight smile.

"With support, I will distract her with support to knock the edge off and then mouth to her to go to her calm place like Mr. Vendetta taught her," Steph replied.

Realization

"Do you think that will work?" Tyson asked.

"Of course. It's just like Mr. Vendetta said. We may not have Diana's power exactly but our words still have power and since we are close with Diana, she will most likely listen to us. We got this," Steph encouraged Tyson.

"Okay..." Tyson said.

An excerpt from Diana's rebuttal:

The shark's home is the ocean, that is their territory. So, while the situation where a person has been attacked by a shark in their territory is a tragedy; how can we demonize sharks to the point of being okay with their extinction when we are the ones invading their territory? Not to say that it was their fault for going into their territory, but when you have a shark that doesn't have very good eyesight that is hungry looking for a weak seal and there is a human in the water, swimming, looking like a flailing seal and the shark attacks the human; how can we be so upset at the shark, that doesn't know any better, going for what they think is their usual dinner? Also, there have been numerous records of evidence that multiple countries that have "so-called" banned shark finning are still stealthily allowing this to occur because their governments are receiving payment from the fishers in the area. So, they certainly are not being protected enough. The slaughtering of 11.5 thousand sharks an hour is not an acceptable number for the population control of any species. However, it is a great feat for extinction records. There are many countries that ban certain food or limit the amount of certain food to their citizens and it is normalized and praised because, usually, those certain animals they are protecting are essential to the environment and sharks would fall into that category...

An excerpt from Hannah's rebuttal.

To put the lives of sharks, of all creatures, over the lives of humans is simply insensitive and demented. By stating that the sharks "cannot help" but to attack what they see as food whether it is a human or a seal only further proves my point that they are vicious killing machines and always looking for a meal. How could a person agree to diminish a person's rights for the sake of sharks? Furthermore, countries do not usually ban certain foods on the grounds of the animals being essential to the environment. They, in fact, usually dictate how certain animals are prepared for consumption, resulting in non-steroid-based strategies. The right of food still stands, regardless if some people want it to or not...

Realization

"Tyson, I think Diana is getting upset. Look," Stephanie said as she pointed to Diana's balled-up fist.

"Yea, Hannah is going really hard on her. She basically made Diana sound like she didn't do her research," Tyson responded.

"We have to get her to come down," Steph said as she began to stand up.

"Wait, you still haven't told me exactly how he will encourage her," Tyson said.

"Just follow my lead," Steph said as Tyson also began to stand.

"Go Diana, you got this girl," Steph yelled.

"Yea, Go Diana Woooooooo woooo," Tyson yelled while clapping very loudly, interrupting the debate.

Seconds after Steph and Tyson interrupted they got met with a stern look from Mr. Kyle as he started to walk down the steps to approach them. Meanwhile, Diana is looking confused. However, her fist started to unclench and when she looked to Steph and Tyson wondering why they did that, she saw them mouthed "Go to your calm place" while Mr. Kyle was too busy giving them a speech to notice.

"I bet you're happy your little friends made that distraction because you were about to be toast. You should do more intensive research like me," Hannah taunted.

"I researched for hours," Diana said.

"Obviously either your laptop is broken or your brain is if you thought that was going to be enough to beat me you little pest," Hannah said.

"You're the one who," Diana said before she clenched her mouth shut.

"Oh no, what was Diana going to say? Use your words Diana. Are you going to just stand there like a little kid? Are you going to..."

Diana heard as she started to tune Hannah out. Her friends told her to go to her calm place and risked not being allowed in the theater again, "I can't blow this," Diana thought to herself. "Think about my room. I'm sitting on my bed snuggled against my stuffed animals in the dark. I see my light up stars on the ceiling and butterflies on the wall. I smell lavender in the air from my candles. I hear blissful silence..." Diana thought to herself. After waiting a few more seconds, letting her heartbeat slow down she decided that she was calm enough to come back to the present.

Realization

When Diana came back to the present she was met with an angered Mr. Kyle, walking, on his way back to them and Hannah standing with her arms folded.

"I'm sorry about that, girls. I can't believe they would interrupt you like that, Hannah," Mr. Kyle said.

"It's okay they just wanted to support their friend, I can understand that. I was almost done anyway," Hannah said.

"I'm so glad you feel that way, Hannah. Due to the disruption, I have to cut this a bit short to keep on schedule with the next teams. But, I will have the competition members sheet posted on the board on Monday. Have a good day, girls. You both are free to go," Mr. Kyle said.

"Bye, Mr. Kyle," both girls said in unison.

Diana and Hannah walked to opposite exits in the auditorium, Diana going towards the door Steph and Tyson went through and Hannah towards the nearest exit to her. When Diana walked through the doors she was met with looks of anticipation.

"Sooo, did you go to your calm place? Did the distraction work?" Steph said, looking like she was biting her nails.

"Yes, I was able to control myself. Thank you guys so much for being there. Who knows what I would have said if you all hadn't done what you did in there," Diana replied.

"Then why do you look so sad? Did you not make it?" Tyson asked.

"No, he is going to put up the list tomorrow. I'm just bummed because she made me out to be an idiot who didn't do enough research. I was humiliated out there," Diana replied.

"You did amazing, especially for it to be your first ever debate", Steph said.

"Yea, Steph is right. I really enjoyed your debate. If I was the judge I'd side with you," Tyson said.

"You all are just saying that because you're my friends and you care about me," Diana said, still with her head down.

"While that is definitely the case, it is also the truth," Steph said, as she pulled her in for a hug, which Tyson joined shortly after.

Meanwhile, at the exit Hannah goes through, Hannah gets a call.

Ring Ring!

"Okay, I got this. I did what I could do. A lot is riding on this," Hannah said to herself right before she answered the phone.

"Hello, Dad," Hannah said.

"Hello, have you completed the task?" He asked.

"Yes, sir," Hannah replied.

"Tell me the report on the subject," He commanded.

"The subject responded well. When I tried to anger her and trigger her powers she withheld her anger and calmed down," Hannah stated.

"That is remarkable, you have proven yourself useful," he said.

"Does that mean you can come home and eat dinner with me tonight?" Hannah asked, hoping he would finally agree.

"No. You know work comes first. Stop asking me. I give you a place to lay your head, designer clothes on your back, and buy you anything you say you want. Is that not enough?" He asked.

"Yes, Dad. I'm sorry I asked."

"Don't ask again," He commanded right before he hung up the phone.

Hannah then calls an Uber to take her home with her head hung low. Later on, that day Diana is still in a funk. Ms. Monroe had tried to cheer her up by playing her favorite songs on the way back to the house but it was no use. Diana was convinced that she had blown her chance of being on the competition team and proving Hannah wrong. After dinner, Ms. Monroe planned to try and get Diana out of her gloom for the final time.

"Hey, my pretty girl, everything is going to be alright. I know you did well and you will make it on the team. I'm your Mom, I know. You are talented, driven, and intelligent. I just know you made it. You need to be more confident in yourself," Ms. Monroe suggested.

"But, you weren't there, Mom. You didn't see just how badly Hannah showed me up. She completely humiliated me in front of Mr. Kyle," Diana said.

"Did anyone laugh? Did Steph and Tyson say you bombed it? No. It's okay to feel disappointed. However, you can't allow yourself to feel that way all day. Emotions are a feeling not a state of being. Why don't you try and do some things that cheer you up? You can do your extreme dot-to-dot or go outside and jump on the trampoline or... Maybe you could-"

"Mom, I really don't feel like doing that right now. I'm just not in the mood right now," Diana interrupted.

Realization

"Baby. You have to try. If you get in the habit of letting one experience that makes you feel down determine the rest of your day, then you will be sad for a longer time. You don't like feeling sad, do you?" Ms. Monroe said.

"No, of course not," Diana said as she began to cry.

"Well, you have to do the things that make you happy in order to get over your funk. I'm not allowing you to wallow in your sadness for too long because I care about you. You've been sad since we were in the car, you have to learn to manage your emotions. You're not meant to be sad forever. Let me help you help yourself. You want me to get you some ice cream? Will that help?"

"I just want you to leave me alone. Why do you have to care so much? Why can't you just leave me alone?" Diana said while bringing her knees to her head.

Then, just like that, Ms. Monroe left Diana alone. After about an hour or so Diana decided she didn't want to feel as sad. So, she took her Mom's advice and started doing her extreme-dot-to-dot and let the time pass her by as she drew and connected the dots on the paper. Eventually, Diana did start to feel better. The weight of what happened wasn't as overwhelming anymore.

She then got dressed for bed. She turned on the nature sounds that made her feel calm and eventually drifted off to sleep.

Meanwhile, Diana's Mom was still lying awake feeling empty. "What is going on with me?" she thought. She felt like something was missing like a disconnection of some sort and it scared her. To take her mind off of it, she decided to read her favorite book until she felt tired enough to fall asleep.

In the morning, Ms. Monroe woke up early by her alarm clock, as usual, and started making breakfast. It was only until she received an update notification on her phone and saw Diana's picture on her lock screen that she noticed the meal she was preparing was only enough for one. She had always made enough for Diana, but today was different. It was as if she completely forgot about Diana, that she wasn't even concerned about her well-being. She knew it was wrong to feel that way. So, she left all the food for Diana and decided to grab something on the way to work after she dropped Diana off at school.

Diana, woken up by her alarm clock, got up and got ready for school. She thought that it was weird that her Mom didn't wake her up this morning, but she figured that she was just upset about last night. She then went downstairs and ate her breakfast. Her Mom was strangely silent, it wasn't like her to hold a grudge, "we're partners, we always make up," Diana thought. In the car, Diana tried to make small talk.

"Hey, how was your morning?" Diana asked.

"It was okay," Ms. Monroe replied.

"Okayy, well my morning was good too," Diana said, hopeful her Mom would show some interest.

"Ummm...are you ready to go to work?" Diana asked after she was met with silence from her last statement.

"Yes, I am," Ms. Monroe.

"Mom, are you mad at me? I really didn't mean what I said. You know that right? I even did what you said and it made me feel better," Diana asked.

"I'm perfectly fine," Ms. Monroe responded.

"Okay," Diana said, not sure how to really understand her response.

When they arrived at the school, Diana got out of the car and started walking to the double doors. She didn't get a hug or a kiss goodbye or even "have a great day at school" from her Mom. She was certain her Mom was upset with her, that was the only reason she would be acting like this. She had to make it up to her somehow.

After dropping Diana off at school, Ms. Monroe was trying to figure out why she couldn't bring herself to kiss her child goodbye or even give her a hug. This frightened her. So, she called her friend, Zachery, to see if he had any ideas.

"Hey, Zach," Ms. Monroe said.

"Hey, darling, what's wrong? I can hear it in your voice," Zach asked.

"You can always tell. Something happened with Diana again," Ms. Monroe responded.

"Oh no. Do I need to see if I can get her to a new school?" Zach asked.

"Ohh, no it's not like what happened last time…or is it? I'm not exactly sure what happened," Ms. Monroe admitted.

"Are you hurt? Do you need me?" Zach asked.

"No, not exactly. I'm actually okay, extremely okay as if I don't care at all," Ms. Monroe said.

"That sounds good to me? Why isn't that a good thing to you?" Zach asked.

"I should care. I should automatically think of my daughter when I wake up. I should be cooking us both breakfast, not just me. I should want to talk to her in the car. I should be concerned with her well-being, but ever since last night, I haven't cared. That scares me. It's like there's a numb section of my heart," Ms. Monroe explained.

"Well tell me what happened last night and maybe I can help...?" Zach asked.

"I don't think you will really be able to help but I'll tell you. Diana was feeling down because she felt like she bombed her mock debate competition and had been sulking all day long. So, I told her that she needed to do some things that would make her feel better. I told her, her feelings are feelings not states of being. I thought I was helping her but she shut me out and told me she wished I didn't care about her and now I don't," Ms. Monroe said.

"That sounds similar to what you had told me about the incidents that happened at the other schools, how she had told them something and it actually happened. I'm not sure what to make of it, but you will be okay. It shouldn't be permanent right?" Zach asked.

"That's the thing. I don't know. I had only heard about what happened to them or witnessed it with my eyes, but I had never actually felt it and it's terrifying, Zach. What if I never get that motherly, worrisome feeling again? I'm scared," Ms. Monroe said while fighting back tears.

"Your daughter is special. She might even be able to reverse it. I think you should tell her how you're feeling," Zach suggested.

"I can't do that. How can I tell my daughter that I don't care for her anymore? I'm the one person, other than her father, that is supposed to care for her. Her Dad is already gone. So, that just leaves me. I can't do that to her. How can I tell my daughter that I'm afraid of what she can do? That...that I'm afraid of her, MMs. Monroe asked, finally letting her tears fall.

"Okay, I see your point there, but we have to think of something unless you just want to wait it out to see if it will go away on its own," Zach said.

"I like that idea better," Ms. Monroe said, wiping away her tears.

"But if it doesn't get any better in three days then you have to talk to her. Or I will talk to her if you'd prefer that, she doesn't really like me like that but she might listen."

"You're sweet but I don't think she'd go for that, but I will wait the three days and see what happens and if it doesn't go away we can discuss other options then. Okay?" Ms. Monroe said.

"Okay, as long as you know I'll always be there for you and Diana," Zach said.

"I know and I love you for that," Ms. Monroe responded with a smile on her face as she sniffled.

"I love you too. I have to go so I won't be late for work. I'll call later to check on you okay?" Zach asked.

"Okay, Bye," Ms. Monroe said.

"Bye," Zach said as he hung up.

When Diana got to school and met up with Steph and Tyson she wasn't able to hide how she was feeling. Steph knew when she saw her face that she wasn't having the best day.

"Hey, what's wrong?" Steph asked after bringing Diana in for a hug.

"My Mom and I had a fight yesterday I guess. She's barely talking to me and she didn't even wake me up this morning or give me a hug goodbye. She's never been this upset with me. I don't know what to do," Diana explained.

"What happened? Why did you all fight?" Steph asked.

"Well, I was feeling really bad about the way the mock debate turned out and my Mom was trying to get me out of my funk, but I wasn't listening to her, it's like I knew what she said would help me so I shut it out because I felt like I should be sad. Then I told her I wish she wouldn't care so much and to leave me alone and she actually left," Diana explained.

"Yeah, sometimes when things happen that make me feel sad I will be sad for a while, and even when my parents try to cheer me up it would work but I'd still feel like I should be sad because I felt like I shouldn't be happy again so close to a time that I was just sad. But I learned that a feeling is just that, a feeling. If someone was to pinch me I'd feel it and it might even linger a bit, but eventually, it goes away and I stop feeling it. Sometimes even when the sad feeling, or disappointment feeling was gone I would still mope around telling myself I should be sad. I had to learn to let things go," Steph said.

"Yeah, that's what my Mom was trying to explain to me and I eventually caught on and I did start to feel better," Diana said.

"But, sometimes the feeling still feels fresh after a long time," Tyson said.

"Well, sometimes the feeling needs some help to go away. You have to do things that make you genuinely happy, for example, my thing that makes me happy is doing extreme dot-to-dot, dancing in my room, and doing karaoke," Diana said.

"I'm not sure what activities make me genuinely happy. What's the difference between happy and genuinely happy?" Tyson asked.

"I would say when you are genuinely happy is when you are able to do something and time simply passes and you don't even feel tired. If you were ever offered to be able to do this task or activity you would always be willing to do it because you really really like it. Things like that," Steph explained.

"Oh, okay that makes sense but there are still going to be times when I don't even want to do those things. What should I do then?" Tyson asked.

"My Mom says when you are really sad and you don't want to do anything are the most important times that you should force yourself to do those things. It's just like if you got a really really bad cut on your skin and you have to go to the doctor to get stitches and special ointment. Big emotional wounds need more help and time to heal. So, it's important for you to help it along by doing things you know that bring you happiness and you have to allow them to work. If you don't have hope that things will get better then the things that usually make you happy probably won't work," Steph explained.

"My Mom also says sometimes you should try to do things out of your comfort zone to see if it helps and there are always adults that can help," Diana added.

"Sometimes adults don't understand and make me feel worse," Tyson added.

"Well, just like there are trained doctors to stitch the cuts there are trained adults that help with emotional wounds like Ms. Abigail, our counselor," Steph said.

"Dang I wish I knew this a while ago. I wasn't always so okay with my parents not being there but I didn't tell anyone because I didn't think anyone could really help with that, but eventually, it got better when I started doing things I liked all day and leaving them notes," Tyson said.

"If you truly do feel better about it now that that's great and if you still feel sad about it you can always talk to us or Ms. Abigail. Her office is five doors down from the front office," Steph suggested.

"Thanks, guys. I'm sorry I got us off-topic. Diana, do you think your powers affected her," Tyson said.

"That's what friends are for and no... I don't think so. I was sad, not mad. Usually, it only works when I'm really angry," Diana said.

"Well, that's not what Mr. Vendetta said when he explained it before. He said any strong emotion and that anger just tends to be one that has the most effect. So, technically it could be your powers since you were very sad when you told her that," Steph countered.

"But even if it was my power that is making her act like this. The effects have never lasted this long before. That can't be it," Diana said.

"Usually you would use your power to stop the effects by saying something else. Did you try that?" Tyson asked.

"No, I didn't. Maybe I should...But what if I mess her up even more. This is my Mom we're talking about. What if I hurt her more?" Diana asked desperately.

"You won't but if you want to consult Mr. Vendetta about it before you try then that may be a good idea," Steph responded

"Yeah, he should definitely know what's going on. I'm confident he does," Tyson said.

"Well, I'll talk to him tomorrow. I don't want to bring this up to him if she ends up fine later on today," Diana said.

"True," Steph and Tyson said simultaneously.

"Hey, isn't today the day Mr. Kyle puts up the list for the competition debate team members?!" Tyson asked.

"Yeah, it is. You should go check. I have a feeling a very special person's name is going to be on it," Steph said.

"Guys...you know I don't like to get my hopes up like that. But I'll go check it out to see," Diana said.

"It's okay to get your hopes up sometimes. I have a good feeling about it. You know my feelings are usually spot on. Also, we have to get to class soon or we will be late. Hurry up," Steph said with a wink.

"The keyword is usually," Diana said as she laughed and walked toward the bulletin board.

"Uhh, whatever I know I'm right," Steph said as she playfully crossed her arms.

"I believe you," Tyson said.

"I know," Steph said while smiling.

Realization

As Diana walks to the board, her heart is racing. Steph did tell her that she had a good feeling so that calmed her a bit. When she arrived, she looked for her last name and there it was! Diana was shocked that she actually made it on the team. She thought for sure that her speech wasn't good enough, but as it turns out she was. She was so excited and the first person she wanted to tell was her Mom, but she didn't even know how to tell her or if she even wanted to hear the news after what happened, but she needed to hurry and get to class and tell Steph and Tyson. "I guess Steph was right as usual," Diana thought to herself with a smile on her face.

When Diana walked into class, she let out a sigh as she heard the bell ring before she went to her seat. By the smile on her face both Steph and Tyson knew she had made it on the team and they shot her a quick thumbs up before she sat down.

The day went on like any other day aside from the uneasiness Diana felt about telling her Mom the good news. Diana made sure to avoid Mr. Vendetta all day so that she wouldn't be tempted to talk to him about the situation and she was almost certain he saw her look at him at one point, but she tried to play it off like she was simply looking at the exit sign directly behind him, hoping it worked.

When the day was over and it was time for Diana to go to the car-rider station, she half expected her Mom not to have shown up but when she peered through the doors she saw the Honda Accord in the line. As she walked to the car, she hoped and hoped that her Mom was back to the way she usually was. When she got inside she was greeted with…

.

"Hey, umm how was your day?" Ms. Monroe said with a shy smile.

"Hey, it was good actually. I have good news," Diana said.

"Okay, she's talking more than I expected. That's a good sign. Something still seems off though," Diana thought to herself.

"Okay, I'm listening," Ms. Monroe said.

"I made the team. You were right. I did better than I thought I did, yayy," Diana said hesitantly with a wide smile.

"Well that's Great Diana," Ms. Monroe replied.

"She barely ever calls me by my real name," Diana thought to herself.

"Yep, sure is, "Diana said.

"We...ummm...We need to talk when we get home okay," Ms. Monroe said.

"Okay," Diana replied.

"Oh no... not another talk when we get home...I hope it turns out just as good as the last time," Diana thought to herself.

The rest of the car ride was filled with silence. Diana knew that that meant this wasn't going to be a pleasant conversation. When they pulled up the hill and got out of the car Diana's heart was pounding.

When they entered the house Diana and Ms. Monroe sat down at the kitchen table. Diana was too nervous to start the conversation...

"Okay ummm... I don't know how to say this, Diana, but we have to get you some help," Ms. Monroe said as her eyes started to water.

"Help for what, Mommy? Why are you about to cry? Is it about what I said yesterday?" Diana said as she held her head down.

"It's not about what you said, Diana. It's about how it made me feel. I know about what happened to the other kids at the other schools but this time I felt it. I- I felt numb to you. It's like your words came true. I just had stopped feeling that way after work today. We have to fix this somehow," Ms. Monroe said as she grabbed Diana's shoulders as tears streamed down her face.

"Mom I have-," Diana started to say.

"I know sweetie. You have a problem, but don't worry we will figure this out and get you better. We will find a doctor and they will fix you. They have to," Ms. Monroe said as she pulled Diana into a tight hug.

"But Mom it's not-" Diana tried to explain.

"Shhhhh. Don't talk baby. I've already decided I'm going to talk to my friend and we will figure something out. I'll make dinner and tomorrow after school we will get this under control," Ms. Monroe said as she put on a fake smile while wiping away her tears, sending Diana upstairs.

"It's useless. She won't listen to me and if I didn't know any better I think she's afraid to let me talk," Diana thought to herself as she sat in her room cuddled under a blanket. "How can I explain to her what's going on if I can't talk? Maybe I can write it down...Nooo, sometimes words written down affect people differently than if I were to say it. Who's to say she would even look at the letter if I did write it down since she's convinced something is wrong with me. Okay, so what should I do? Maybe Mr. Vendetta can help. Maybe he can explain it like how he explained it to me. Yes, I'll get him to come over," Diana concluded in her head.

Later that day, Diana decided she wouldn't speak during dinner to make her Mom feel more at ease and it seemed to work. Meanwhile, Diana was thinking about why the effects didn't wear off as fast as before. "Is my power getting stronger?" Diana pondered in her head. Before bed, she decided to meditate to clear her mind after everything that happened that day. She turned off her main light, turned on her Himalayan Salt lamp, cut on her soothing music, and closed her eyes while focusing on being in the moment, breathing, and how her body was feeling. She meditated for about fifteen minutes and then she prepared for bed and she was able to fall asleep quite easily.

It was the next morning and things started to return to normal other than Diana still thinking it was best for her not to speak for the sake of her mother. On the car ride to school, her Mom continued to talk about how she and her friend will find someone who could help Diana while the radio played in the background. Diana knew that her Mom needed to talk about it to make herself feel better. So, it didn't really bother Diana. She, instead, focused on the hope that Mr. Vendetta would be able to explain her power to her Mom to calm her down.

When Diana got to school, she immediately started to look for Mr. Vendetta. She knew if she could get to him early enough she could tell him what's going on and it would go smoothly. The first place she visited was his office and low and behold he was in there drinking coffee.

"I knew I'd be seeing you around here soon since I saw you avoiding me yesterday," Mr. Vendetta said.

"Ohhh, you saw that huh," Diana said with a wide smile with her hand behind her head.

"Yes, I'm very attentive. As a janitor, I have to pay attention and keep my eyes peeled for any messes that have already happened and those yet to happen," Mr. Vendetta said confidently.

"Really?" Diana said with a little sarcasm and a chuckle.

"You bet," Mr. Vendetta said with a thumbs up.

"That's really cheesy, you know that right?" Diana said.

Realization

"I know. It just looked like you needed a laugh, but enough of me hopelessly trying to be a comedian. I take it that my jokes weren't the reason you came. I'm guessing it's about whatever you were thinking about telling me yesterday but instead avoided me?" Mr. Vendetta implied.

"Yeah, righhhtt. You see, my Mom has experienced the effects of my powers first-hand and it's freaking her out. She doesn't even want me to speak and she is getting her friend to take me to some doctor so they can *fix* me. Can you help?" Diana pleaded.

"I didn't think she'd react like that. I can umm give you a few pointers on how to explain it so she can understand it better," Mr. Vendetta replied.

"No no, I need *you* to talk to her, Mr. Vendetta," Diana insisted.

"I don't know if that will be a good idea," Mr. Vendetta said nervously.

"You have to, she won't listen to me, but she will to you. You're the expert on this. You have to," Diana pleaded.

Ding Dong! Ding Dong!

"Oh no I'm late. Mr. Vendetta, please help me. If I go to this doctor, they might out me to everyone or run tests on me pleaseee," Diana begged.

"More than likely the doctor wouldn't even believe your Mom," Mr. Vendetta retorted.

"More than likely isn't one hundred percent please?" Diana asked

"Okay, okay. I'll do it. Let me write you a note for class," Mr. Vendetta responded.

"You can do that?" Diana asked.

"Yes, as a matter of fact, I can. I do have some authority being the janitor," Mr. Vendetta said proudly.

"Well, thank you. I'll see you at my house before 6:00," Diana said happily.

"I'll be there," Mr. Vendetta said softly as Diana left his office.

When Diana got to class she was scolded for being late, of course, but after she handed Mr. Campbell the note he read it and said, "Oh, I'm sorry Miss Monroe. It was nice of you to help Mr. Vendetta clean. Go ahead and get to your seat. Today, we are learning about fossil fuels," before he started his lecture. As Diana walked to her seat both Steph and Tyson looked at her with worry. So, she gave them a small thumbs up to assure them everything was okay. Once they got to lunch, Steph and Tyson started with their questions that they had been holding in since that morning.

"So, is your Mom feeling better now?" Steph asked.

"She isn't feeling the effects anymore. Now she is just scared which I'm not so certain is a step up," Diana replied.

"Is she still too scared for you to talk?" Tyson asked.

"Yes, well I guess she is. I haven't talked around her to test that out yet, but I'm pretty sure she is," Diana replied.

"How are you doing? Sorry, that wasn't our first question," Steph asked.

"I'm okay. I'm better now that Mr. Vendetta agreed to talk to my Mom tonight before she and her friend take me to this doctor so he can *fix* me," Diana explained.

"What do you mean, fix you?" Tyson said.

"Those were my Mom's exact words. She doesn't understand my power and she's too afraid to hear what I have to say when I explain it to her. That's why I went ahead and asked Mr. Vendetta to talk to her for me," Diana said.

"Well, that's probably for the best," Steph said.

"Yeah, it was. Mr. Vendetta is the ultimate expert," Tyson assured them.

"Yeah, he's the one that explained it to me. So, it only made sense for me to ask him," Diana said.

"I'm glad, so she won't take you to the doctor," Steph said.

"Would the doctor even believe her if she brought you there anyway?" Tyson asked.

"Well, from what I understand my power doesn't physically affect me in a way that the doctor could actually see, but who's to say my cells aren't different from yours," Diana said.

"It would be bad if they started doing experiments on you and found a way to weaponize your power," Steph said.

"Could they really do that? Wouldn't Diana have to say the words they need when they want her to? Right?" Tyson asked.

"Technology has really advanced. There's no telling what they could do," Diana said.

"Okay, let's not spiral because there are endless possibilities, "Steph said.

"Yeah, Steph. Saying there are endless possibilities isn't really helpful," Tyson said.

"Okay let's change the subject…" Diana said while twirling her fork around her food.

"We haven't hung out in a while and we haven't celebrated you getting on the team, Diana," Tyson said.

"That's right! We haven't celebrated yet. Let's hang out this weekend!" Steph said.

"You guys can come over to my house," Tyson said.

"Are your parents going to be there? My parents are very strict about that," Steph said.

"My Mom is too," Diana added.

"I know. My uncle is going to come be with me this weekend so an adult can be there. He comes over and we play video games a few times a month," Tyson said.

"Okay, sounds like a plan," Steph said with a bright smile.

"This weekend it is," Diana said with a grin.

The rest of the day, Diana was hoping Mr. Vendetta would pull through for her. She tried to focus on her assignments but she just couldn't. Luckily, the assignments weren't officially due until the next day. So, she had some time. When the final bell rang,

Diana ran to Mr. Vendetta's office to make sure he remembered to come over and he gave her a thumbs up with a wide smile to reassure her. Then she made her way to the car riders and waited for her Mom to come around the corner before she hopped in and commenced the ride of silence.

When Diana got home, she went upstairs to her room and cracked her door in order to listen out for when Mr. Vendetta got there. Ms. Monroe prepared dinner so Diana could have a full stomach before they took her to the doctor because she didn't know how long they would be there. As she put the casserole into the oven she heard the doorbell ring.

"Is Zachery here?" Ms. Monroe thought to herself as she went to the door

"I can't really see who it is," Ms. Monroe thought.

"Who is it?" Ms. Monroe yelled through the door.

"I'm Mr. Vendetta. I'm the janitor at Pedita Middle School," Mr. Vendetta responded through the door.

"What the…" Ms. Monroe thought to herself.

"COMING!" Diana yelled as she ran down the stairs.

"Diana, what are you doing? We don't know this man. He could be a crazy person or-" Ms. Monroe started to say.

"Mom, I invited him over to talk to you," Diana explained.

"You don't just invite someone over to my house. That's dangerous," Ms. Monroe scolded.

"But, he's already here. Aren't you going to let him in?" Diana asked.

"Fine...but don't ever do that again, you understand me?" Ms. Monroe instructed.

"Yes, Ma'am," Diana happily replied.

"One second sir, it's a complicated lo.." Ms. Monroe started to say as she opened the door.

"Hey, Mr. Vendetta thank you for coming," Diana said as she gave him a big hug.

"Diana. Go upstairs," Ms. Monroe instructed in a stern tone.

"But why," Diana started to say before.

"I won't repeat myself, now go upstairs to your room and close the door," Ms. Monroe said.

"Yes ma'am," Diana said as she headed upstairs confused.

Ms. Monroe and Mr. Vendetta just stared at each other in awkward silence. The tension could be felt through the air. As soon as Ms. Monroe heard Diana's door closed, she started to speak.

"Mr. Vendetta? That's what you go by now? Why are *you* here? Why are *you*, of all people, at my house? Why now and how do you know Diana?" Ms. Monroe asked while trying to contain herself.

"I've been helping her at school. I work there as a janitor," Mr. Vendetta replied.

"Helping her with what? Why are you speaking to her? I don't want you talking to her anymore. Why have you inserted yourself in her life? Did you think that when I found out I'll be happy that you finally resurfaced? Well, I'm not. I want nothing to do with you and you need to leave right now," Ms. Monroe said while trying to hold back her tears.

"Please don't cry Alli-cat," Mr. Vendetta said as he stepped closer to her and reached out.

"You don't have the right to call me that anymore...and do not touch me, Dad...or should I say *Mr. Vendetta*," Ms. Monroe.

"I'm sorry," Mr. Vendetta said as he backed away.

"I believe I told you to leave," Ms. Monroe said as she crossed her arms waiting for him to turn and leave.

"I can't...until we talk," Mr. Vendetta said.

"Oh, yes you can. This is my house and you aren't welcome here," Ms. Monroe said.

"It's about Diana's power or should I say condition," Mr. Vendetta said.

"Wait, how do you know about that?" Ms. Monroe asked.

"I've been helping her with it at school," Mr. Vendetta explained.

"Well, the doctors can do that when we get there. You are no longer needed," Ms. Monroe.

"No. You *can't* do that," Mr. Vendetta urged strongly.

"I am her *mother* and I'm in charge of her, not you. Just because you are her grandfather by blood doesn't mean anything. You weren't there for me and you haven't been there for Diana. So, I'm going to take *my* daughter to the doctor so they can fix her condition," Ms. Monroe said.

"She does not need fixing. She has power," Mr. Vendetta said.

"Well that *power* causes trouble and that needs to stop and I'm hoping a doctor will be able to fix it. They have to," Ms. Monroe said.

"Her words have power," Mr. Vendetta said.

"I know. I felt it first hand," Ms. Monroe said sternly.

"And you're scared," Mr. Vendetta said.

"No... I am not. That's preposterous," Ms. Monroe said as she tapped her foot.

"You are not a very good liar. Diana gets that from you and you got that from your mother. I know all your tells," Mr. Vendetta said.

"Well, you sure never had a problem with it," Ms. Monroe retorted.

"You don't understand," Mr. Vendetta said as he sat down at the table.

"What don't I understand? Explain it to me, Dad," Ms. Monroe said.

"As I said Diana's words have power, but so does everyone's," Mr. Vendetta explains.

"The last time I checked when I told someone to stop talking they didn't literally lose the capability to speak," Ms. Monroe retorted.

"I wasn't finished. Diana's power grows stronger when her emotions are involved. The worst is anger, next is sadness, then fear, and so on. *But* she has the ability to control it. I've seen it. I've been teaching her how to manage her emotions to help her with that. There is no need for a doctor. That would not be a good idea. You do not want her to turn into a spectacle, do you?" Mr. Vendetta asked.

"So, how did you become an expert in this power huh?" Ms. Monroe asked.

"I too have this power," Mr. Vendetta said nervously.

"Wait, so this is genetic? But how can that be? *I* don't have the power...?" Ms. Monroe asked.

"It always skips a generation. I had a feeling Diana's would develop. So, I made sure to get a job as a janitor at her school. I used my government connections to figure out where you were sending the two after she got kicked out. I also made sure that those incidents were taken off her record," Mr. Vendetta explained.

"If you expect me to give you a hug and say thank you then you are mistaken. Have you ever used that on me? Is that why you left?" Ms. Monroe asked.

"We aren't talking about me right now," Mr. Vendetta said.

"You are going to answer my questions since you decided to show your face here," Ms. Monroe said sternly.

"Okay. No, I have never used my power on you. It doesn't work like that and, simply put, yes it was why I had to leave," Mr. Vendetta said.

"What do you mean, *had to*? Oh, so you expect me to believe that you walked out on Mom and me because you were forced to? And how does it work then if not on purpose?" Ms. Monroe asked.

"I don't have permission to tell you. All I can say is that I used to work for the government and they told me I had to leave and the emotions have to be genuine in order for it to work. I cannot and Diana cannot simply tell people to do something. Sometimes things happen that we don't intend to but that's why I'm here, to make her aware of that and help guide her and be there for her since no one was for me," Mr. Vendetta explained.

"I understand now and if you think that just because you revealed this to me that I forgive you for walking out on us, I don't. I also don't want you teaching my daughter. Look where it left you. It forced you to leave your family for who knows why but most certainly can't be good. It all led to you pretending to be a janitor at your granddaughter's school...Need I say more?" Ms. Monroe asked.

"I am the only one that can help her and not corrupt her. She needs me," Mr. Vendetta said sternly.

"So did I... and you left. How can I know that you won't do that to Diana or how can I know that the government won't take her too huh?" Mr. Vendetta.

"I understand the terrible mistake that I made leaving you and your mother. I have to live with that and so much more every day, but I am helping her because I don't want them to get to my granddaughter like they did me. Diana is powerful, even more powerful than me. She doesn't understand everything yet and the dangers of this power, what the government can do. I have been on the inside. I can protect her. Please, I know I give you no reason to trust me, but I will not fail Diana as I did you." As Mr. Vendetta watched his daughter wipe away the single tear that escaped, he hoped she would be able to see past his mistakes to allow him to help. She didn't really understand what was at stake.

"Fine but *only* because Diana needs you. This doesn't change anything between us. Now, what exactly can the government do to her?" Ms. Monroe asked, getting straight to business.

"They have technology that can make her believe something has happened that would stir up emotion which will cause her to say certain words and record her saying them. It's- It's torture," Mr. Vendetta said.

"So, the tapes have the same effect as when she just says it in person?" Ms. Monroe asked.

"No... weaker but in Diana's case, it would still be very powerful, more powerful than mine. They used my tapes for things that I cannot say other than that it would be a malicious act," Mr. Vendetta explained.

"So, it's similar to listening to a radio host and being persuaded to feel a certain way about a topic?" Ms. Monroe asked, trying to better understand what makes these tapes so dangerous.

"Yes, similar to that, but as you know Diana can make people feel some kind of way and make people physically do things, quite literally. So, if they trick her to command things then, Diana will most likely make people do whatever, feel whatever she says, unlike my tapes that only put the suggestion in people's minds or made them feel uneasy or a little pain. That's why it's important for me to shield her from the government. You have done a good job of not causing a spectacle. So, I'm certain they do not know of her power. That gives us a leg up on them," Mr. Vendetta explained.

"I'm guessing we need to keep all recording devices away from her then. Have you told her anything about this yet?"

"No, I have not. I haven't told her about our family relation or about the tapes. I do not wish to scare her. Fear is an emotion that is quite unpredictable and I haven't deemed it necessary for her to know at the moment. Lying is another thing Diana has to look out for because that is her kryptonite as one might say, but she has been an honest girl for now so she doesn't need to know about it. Certain things will need to be brought up and discussed when the time is right, but only then," Mr. Vendetta said.

"Okay, but I don't like lying to my daughter. We are a team, always have been. It doesn't feel right," Ms. Monroe said.

"She will find out when she needs to know. For right now, she doesn't. Hopefully, since the government doesn't know about her yet, she won't need to know for a very long time," Mr. Vendetta said.

"Hopefully...I will tell my friend that we won't be going to the doctor this evening," Ms. Monroe said as she escorted Mr. Vendetta to the door.

"Well, then my job here is done. It was truly nice to see you in person, Ali-cat," Mr. Vendetta said as he tipped his hat and left out the door.

"Bye, Dad," Ms. Monroe said, unsure of how to respond.

"Diana!" Mrs. Monroe yelled upstairs.

"Yes, coming!" Diana yelled back as she raced downstairs.

"Did Mr. Vendetta leave already," Diana asked as she looked around.

"Yes, he has. You don't have to worry about going to the doctor today. I understand now and I'm so sorry sweetheart," Ms. Monroe said as she pulled Diana in for a hug.

"It's okay, I get why you were going to do it. It's really nice to hear you call me sweetheart again," Diana said as she squeezed Ms. Monroe tightly.

"You will always be my sweetheart," Ms. Monroe said.

"Well your sweetheart is ready to eat some casserole," Diana said with a bright smile.

"Oh, goodness," Ms. Monroe said as she ran to the oven to grab the casserole.

"Whew! It didn't burn. I had completely forgotten about it, Diana," Ms. Monroe said as she placed it on the table.

"Well, you know I didn't. Let's eat!" Diana said.

"Okay, let's eat," Ms. Monroe said as she sat down to eat.

That night, Diana was able to sleep soundly, knowing that her mother really understood her power. She didn't have to hide anymore. Although she was a bit confused about why her Mom forced her to go upstairs for the intervention, but as long as it worked, she was okay with it. The next morning Diana woke up to the smell of bacon, eggs, and toast her Mother was preparing downstairs. Diana went ahead and got dressed for school and went to the kitchen table to eat.

"Hey, baby girl. I just wanted to apologize again for how I handled the situation," Ms. Monroe said with a heavy head.

"I can't really blame you for that. Having powers is not normal, but I do forgive you. I'm happy that you know everything along with Stephanie and Tyson," Diana said.

"I should have acted differently. It is always better to be calm in situations like these because then you know you are confronting it with a leveled head to make the best decisions possible. I should have waited until I was calm to try and make decisions on your behalf about your power. I let my fear get the better of me. But even they knew before me?" Ms. Monroe asked.

"Yeah, I feel like I've heard that saying before. I can't remember where I heard it but they've known basically ever since I found out what it was," Diana said with a nervous smile.

"How come I didn't know until now," Ms. Monroe said.

"I wasn't sure if you'd even believe me. If I would have come up to you and said- Mom guess what? I have a superpower- would you have believed me.... truly," Diana asked.

"I guess you have a point there, but from now on I want to be kept abreast of everything too," Ms. Monroe said.

"Definitely. Speaking of my friends, me and Steph are supposed to hang out at Tyson's house with his uncle, is that okay?" Diana asked her.

"You know I don't like last minute things. How old is his uncle?" Ms. Monroe asked.

"I know but I couldn't have asked you before because of you not really wanting me to speak so I figured I'd wait until after Mr. Vendetta talked to you to ask and he is grown, I'm not really sure of his exact age though," Diana said.

"You make yet another valid point. This time you may go. I'll drop you off at 4:00 and pick you up at 8:30, okay?" Ms. Monroe asked

"Yes, thank you, Mommy," Diana said with an exaggerated smile.

"You're welcome. You need to make sure you finish your homework before you go," Ms. Monroe said.

"Of course, I've already started. I only have a little bit left to go. I'll finish it after breakfast," Diana said.

"Okay, as long as it gets done," Ms. Monroe said.

Hours later, after Diana had finished her homework, it was time for them to head to Tyson's house. Diana was excited to tell Steph and Tyson about how well the intervention must have gone for her and her Mom's relationship to be back to normal. Ms. Monroe and Diana jammed to Alessia Cara in the car on the way to Tyson's house. "Wow, I don't think I'd ever get used to pulling up to his house," Diana thought to herself as she stared out the window.

"I'm going to need to speak with his uncle before I go," Ms. Monroe said.

"Okay, I'll go in and tell Tyson," Diana said as she got out of the car.

Diana had never actually been inside Tyson's house before, she'd only been there to drop him off. So, when Tyson opened the door to let her in and she was met with a crystal chandelier, a grand dining room with its *own* chandelier, and the start of a living room with a couch that was as big as her room, she could only stand in awe.

"You can walk in farther, you know. My Mom just says everyone has to take off their shoes because you don't want to track any germs from outside in the room or on the carpet," Tyson said.

"Yeah...my Mom has the same rule," Diana said as she took off her shoes, still in awe.

After a few seconds go by, Diana remembered her Mom was still outside.

"Oh. My Mom wants to meet your uncle that'll be watching us. She's outside in the car," Diana said.

"Okay. Uncle David! Diana's Mom wants to talk to you," Tyson yelled upstairs.

"Okay, I'm coming," David yelled back downstairs.

"Come on, Diana, Steph is already in the common room," Tyson said.

"Okay, lead the way please," Diana said after the shock fully set in.

When they walked into the room and Steph saw Diana, they both started to smile and ran to each other and shared a hug.

"We just saw each other yesterday," Tyson said with a little chuckle.

"Soooo," Diana and Steph said in unison as they continued to hug.

"Okay, so what should we do?" Steph asked after they stopped hugging.

"I, for one, want to know how the talk went with Mr. Vendetta," Tyson said.

"Oh, yes, how did it go? Good I suppose since you don't look sad or like you had gotten tests run on you by freaky doctors," Steph asked.

"Well I wasn't able to hear the conversation but it had to have gone well because my Mom fully understands my power now and even apologized to me," Diana replied.

"Wait, why weren't you able to hear or be there for the convo?" Steph asked.

"Once Mr. Vendetta got there, she told me I had to go to my room and close the door," Diana explained.

"That sounds weird. Don't you think so, Tyson," Steph asked.

"Yeah. You're the one who actually knows who Mr. Vendetta is and the conversation was about *your* powers. So, it doesn't make sense for you to not be there," Tyson said.

"So, the question is...Why would your Mom immediately send you upstairs?" Steph said.

"I mean maybe she still didn't trust Mr. Vendetta. Or she felt like it was a conversation for adults," Diana said.

"The only thing I can possibly think of is that they *do* know each other," Steph said.

"Why do you think that?" Tyson asked.

"Well, for one I have my gut feeling, and two it's because what else could it be? If she knew him and he did her wrong somehow in the past then she wouldn't want Diana to be around him," Steph said.

"Well if that's the case wouldn't her Mom have forbidden Diana to see him anymore if he did her so wrong?" Tyson asked.

"I guess you have a point but I still stand by my theory," Steph said.

"Okay...well he must be someone she knows that did something bad but also someone that she can't afford to not allow him to be in my life and help me," Diana said.

"Okay, okay. I think we're onto something here," Tyson said.

"What kinds of people are people that a person can't afford to lose?... I got it. It makes perfect sense," Steph said as she patted herself on the back.

"Would you like to share with us your thoughts?" Tyson said playfully.

"He must be family. When he found out about Diana's powers and didn't freak out or tell on her or try to run a test, no offense to your Mom, Diana. What random person would act that way to this situation or react so calmly," Steph said.

"Well I never heard of a Vendetta in my family before," Diana said.

"What is your Mom's maiden name?" Tyson asks.

"It's Monroe," Diana replied.

"Okay well, he's not her grandfather," Tyson said.

"Well, he could have always changed his name or something. We need to dig for more information," Steph said.

"Yeah, we do, but them being related makes the perfect sense when you think about it especially because of their powers," Tyson says.

"Mr. Vendetta certainly has a way with his words and has been able to help Diana with her emotions. So, it really does make perfect sense. But we can't determine anything else until we get proof," Steph said.

"Until then, do y'all want to talk about anything else? To take our mind off this? We are basically at a dead end," Tyson asked the group.

"Yeah, that would probably be best," Steph said.

"Yeah, we should," Diana agreed.

"Steph, how is your art going? Are you still thinking of pursuing it as a career?" Tyson asked.

"Actually, yes I am. I had talked to Mr. Vendetta and he gave me things to work on to help with my confidence so that way if some people were to dislike my paintings then I wouldn't feel as bad because I'd *know* that my paintings are great," Steph replied.

"Look at Mr. Vendetta. Always helping out as always, I can't imagine him actually doing something so bad to make my Mom upset," Diana said.

"Everyone has a past, Diana," Steph said.

"True," Diana said,

"What career are you thinking about, Tyson? Are you thinking about becoming a doctor like your parents?" Steph asked.

"I'm not sure yet but I'm pretty certain I don't want to be a doctor," Tyson replied.

"Why not?" Diana asked.

"I can't see myself doing it honestly, it's not my cup of tea," Tyson said.

"Fair enough," Steph said.

"What do you want to be, Diana? Do you want to be a lawyer?" Tyson asked.

"Why did you peg me as a future lawyer?" Diana asked.

"Well, you're on the debate team. So, you're good with arguing and proving your point. Lawyers do that too, right?" Tyson said.

"I see your point. But no, I don't think so. I'm still wrestling between a veterinarian and a teacher like my Mom," Diana said.

"That's a tough one. I could honestly see you as both," Steph said.

"Same here," Tyson said.

"I guess time will tell," Diana said.

"Hey, you guys I cooked dinner and- Did I interrupt anything?" David asked.

"No, you're good. We were just talking about future careers," Tyson replied.

"Well if you wish to know what *my* profession is I'm an intelligence analyst. I work for the government," David said with his hands placed on his hips.

The kids immediately look at each other with the same thought in mind. *This is our chance.*

"So, umm, that means you can access any kind of information like, I don't know, family records?" Steph asked as she showed him a very convincing smile.

"Yes, I suppose I could but usually I am accessing files to help catch bad guys," David said.

"Interesting. Do you happen to have your equipment here?" Diana asked.

"Yesss...What are you guys getting at?" David asked.

"Can you look up a person for us? Please, please, for me?" Tyson begged.

"I can't do that. I could lose my job," David said.

"Pleaseeeeee," Both Diana and Steph said, showing off their puppy eyes.

"I suppose while I can't personally look up this information you guys want to know. *But,* if my little nephew steals my laptop that's in the next room with the password *Candycorn*, and searches for the information on his own, there is nothing I could do about it," David said with a smirk.

"Thank You! Thank you," they all responded in unison.

"Just please don't go crazy and get me in trouble. I need my job," David said.

"You can count on me," Tyson said.

"Okay, let's go to the room now to search the computer," Steph said eagerly.

The kids run to the next room and see the red computer on the desk. Tyson sits in the chair and turns it on and inputs the password. At that point, Diana and Steph got discouraged because Tyson stopped typing.

"Aww man, he can't tell us how the system works or where to even find the information. We're stuck," Diana said with her head hung low.

"Oh, ye of little faith, just give me a second to think. I've got this. It can't be too difficult because he would have told me more information than just the password," Tyson said.

"Or it could be insanely difficult and that's why he's letting us mess around with it in the first place," Steph retorted.

"He wouldn't do that to me. He's not that kind of person and *plus*, he is an intelligence analyst, not a spy, it won't be that difficult…Ahh see," Tyson said. He found the server that appears to be a way to look up people's names.

"You did it!" Steph said while clapping her hands and smiling.

"Well, search it, search his name!" Diana insisted.

"Just to be clear, I don't know exactly what this search engine is really for so don't be too disappointed if his name doesn't show up. I can try another one," Tyson explained.

"Okay, search it already," Steph said as she grew more impatient by the minute.

"Okay, okay. Wait, does anyone know his first name?" Tyson asked with a wide smile.

"Dang it. Do you think it will work similar to Google and we can just search Vendetta, janitor, and middle school?" Diana asked.

"That might work. I'll try it," Tyson said as he tried putting it in the engine.

Realization

As the screen loaded, Steph, Tyson, and Diana could only hold their breath and hope that Mr. Vendetta would come up. Tyson didn't want to admit it but this was probably the only engine he could really find unless he tried to hack the computer but that could get David in trouble. So, this was their only shot.

Luckily, for them, Mr. Vendetta did pop up...six Vendettas actually. They started looking through the choices and picking out the ones that couldn't possibly be him.

"Kimberly Vendetta? No... Kenny Vendetta. No, he's eighteen, and Mr. Vendetta is certainly not eighteen years old. How about Nathan Vendetta? He's 6'2.-6'3 and has black hair. Click on him," Steph said.

"It looks like this is our Vendetta alright, it says he works at Pedita Middle School," Tyson said.

"Does it have a family tab?" Diana asked.

"I'm sure it does. I just need to find it," Tyson said as he started to read all the tabs.

"Check that one," Steph said, pointing to the tab that read *Sealed Records.*

"I really don't think we should. We are already invading his privacy by searching for him," Diana said.

"I'm telling you, my gut is telling me you should look there," Steph insisted.

"I meannnn we *are* already invading his privacy and it might be the reason your Mom was afraid of you being around him in there," Tyson said while looking at Diana.

"Okay, I guess it wouldn't hurt," Diana hesitantly said. She just hoped they wouldn't regret this later.

"So, there are four files but three have been blacked out," Tyson said.

"Well can you do some techy stuff to allow us to see it?" Steph asked.

"I'm pretty sure that means that this information is above my uncle's clearance and if I were to hack it to try and read it then I would most likely get caught and get him in trouble. I've never cracked a government server and I don't think I should go that far. But hey, at least there's one that isn't blacked out," Tyson explained.

"Yeah, you probably shouldn't then. Let's check out the file," Steph said.

"So, it looks like it's a name change. But why would that be in a sealed records tab? I thought name changes are public record," Tyson asked.

"They are public. So, he had this sealed on purpose. He's hiding something. What did his name used to be?" Steph said.

"Yeah, what was his name?" Diana asked.

"It was…Jason Monroe," Tyson said slowly, looking up at Diana and Steph.

"You were right. He must be my grandfather," Diana said. She couldn't believe what she was seeing.

"Why would he keep something like this away from you though?" Steph said.

"Probably the same reason he had to change his name and why these records are sealed," Tyson said.

"True but why wouldn't my Mom tell me. She always tells me everything," Diana said.

"Has she ever talked about her Dad before?" Steph asked.

"No, not really. When I was little and had to do a family tree project and I asked her about him, all she told me was that he was tall with black hair, so I could draw him, but nothing bad about him," Diana said.

"Well, our investigation was successful. I'm sorry that means that Mr. Vendetta and your Mom are keeping something from you," Tyson said as he was about to close the laptop.

"Wait. Does that say *active* over there?" Steph said as she pointed to the bottom right corner of the page.

"What does active mean?" Diana asked.

"Maybe he works for the government too. I mean it makes sense, he is really gifted," Steph said.

"But that would mean that he is lying to me about two things. That he is my grandfather and spying on me for the government," Diana said.

"It might just be a thing that means he's still alive and well. We don't want to jump to conclusions. We don't have all the facts," Tyson said.

"I get you're trying to spare my feelings but come on! This is a government website, he has sealed records that include a name change, just somehow happened to be at the school I end up attending after I changed schools twice already. He's an expert on my power, he probably doesn't even care about me," Diana said, getting frustrated. *How could I be fooled so badly by my own family?*

"Diana, remember to go to your calm place. It's not good for you to get upset," said Steph, putting her hands on her shoulders trying to get her to sit down.

"I don't want to. You know who taught me how to get to my calm place? Mr. Vendetta, the same man that has been lying to me since the very first day he met me. 'm his granddaughter and he didn't even tell me. Don't I deserve to be upset about that for two seconds without someone being scared of me or telling me to calm down?" Diana said as tears started to stream from her eyes.

"It's okay. We are here for you and we aren't scared of you," Steph said as she pulled Diana in for a hug.

"We have your back. You're our friend," Tyson added as he inserted himself into the hug.

"I heard her yell. Is everything okay?" David asked from the doorway.

"Yeah, she will be fine," Steph said as she wiped the edge of her eyes.

"Okayy...Well, I cooked some stir fry for you all. So, come over when you're ready," David said.

"Okay, we'll be over soon," Tyson said.

When David left, Diana started to pull herself together, so David wouldn't ask her any more questions that would make her start crying again. Steph had convinced Diana to give her Mom the rest of the weekend to tell her on her own before she confronted her and Diana agreed to it. Tyson left the room first to set up the table and silverware for Steph and Diana.

Once they all finished the food, they went back to the common room and Diana and Steph waited on their parents. However, before their parents got there they all fell asleep on the couch which made for a cute but hilarious picture that David was able to capture on camera and send to Tyson's parents when he had gone to tell them their parents were there.

Neither Steph nor Diana felt like waking all the way up so Mr. Ansberry carried Steph to the car while Ms. Monroe carried Diana to the car. Ms. Monroe thought Diana was exhausted, but in reality, Diana didn't have anything to say to her and used her sleepiness as a cover to not have to speak to her. She also didn't want to say anything that she didn't mean out of anger and sadness like last time and use her power again.

When the Monroe's got home, Diana walked sleepily to her bedroom and threw her pajamas on, and went straight to sleep, or so her Mom thought. Diana actually laid awake for a while until she drifted off to sleep thinking about everything she found out earlier. Meanwhile, Ms. Monroe went to bed with a clear head, completely unaware that her daughter knew the truth about her father.

Realization

It was the next morning and Ms. Monroe was already preparing breakfast and Diana sat at the table silent as a mouse.

"Okay, what is it, sweetheart?" Ms. Monroe asked.

"Nothing. I'm perfectly fine," Diana said.

"What's with the attitude? Did something happen at Tyson's house? Is there something you want to tell me?" Ms. Monroe said.

"Is there something you want to tell me...Mom?" Diana asked angrily.

"I don't appreciate that tone! I'm your Mother and you will not talk to me like that!" Ms. Monroe demanded.

"Exactly you're my *Mom*. Why wouldn't you tell me?" Diana said as tears started to stream down her face.

"What- what are you talking about you...you have to be more specific," Ms. Monroe said nervously.

"I know...I know who Mr. Vendetta is.... or should I say, Jason Monroe," Diana said.

"How-," Ms. Monroe started to say.

"How did I find out that you lied to me? That *he's* been lying to me since the day I met him. Were you ever going to tell me?" Diana asked.

"I just didn't feel like it was the right time for-" Ms. Monroe started to say.

"So, you weren't going to tell me?" Diana said.

"I just- No I wasn't going to tell you," Ms. Monroe admitted.

"Why? What did he do that made you not want him to be in my life? For me not to meet my own Grandfather?" Diana asked.

"He left us. He left me and my Mother. I didn't even know where he was until now," Ms. Monroe explained.

"But that doesn't explain why you didn't tell me. If he's back, why not tell me?" Diana asked.

"Because I don't have to explain myself to you. I had my reasons," Ms. Monroe said.

"Mom, please," Diana begged.

"I didn't want for you to get attached to him and for him to leave you too. I was looking out for you. I didn't want you to get hurt like me," Ms. Monroe said, her eyes watery with tears.

"By lying to me. You should have told me. You always tell me not to lie. To be honest, all the books say honesty is the best policy but *you* lied to me. You said lying is never okay, that your word is everything," Diana said.

Realization

"I know what I told you and it's true it really is. But sometimes in certain situations-" Ms. Monroe said.

"What are the criteria for when it's the right time to lie? I thought lying is wrong no matter the circumstance?" Diana asked.

"You'll understand when you get older. All I can say now is that I'm sorry for not telling you."

Diana didn't have anything else to say so she went upstairs and cried herself to sleep. She didn't even come down to eat when Ms. Monroe had made her favorite. Ms. Monroe also questioned herself on if she had made the right decision to keep that from her.

"I was doing the right thing. Of course, I was…not. I can't tell her to be a person of her word if I'm not going to be a person of mine. Lying from omission is just the same even if I determine it was for good reason. It hurt her when I could have told the truth and she probably would've been excited. I was too afraid of what could happen instead of being open-minded and giving my Dad a chance to do better than he was with me. I mean he has been consistent so far. Maybe I was too upset with him because of what he did that I ignored what he's been doing. He has helped her a lot. She hasn't had a major situation since being at Pedita. So, he must be doing something right. Yea I really messed up. I need to make it up to her and really apologize."

"I'll go do that now," Ms. Monroe said as she walked upstairs toward Diana's room.

"Hey, can we~," Ms. Monroe started to say as she started to walk into the room and noticed Diana sleeping and slowly started to close the door, not to wake her.

"I'll wake her up early tomorrow so we can talk," Ms. Monroe said to herself.

It was the next morning and Ms. Monroe woke up extra early and made breakfast, preparing for the talk that awaited her. When the food was done and the table was set she went upstairs to wake Diana.

"Hey, sweetie, I need you to wake up. We need to talk. I've made breakfast," Ms. Monroe announced before she closed the door and headed back downstairs.

Diana thought about pretending that she was still asleep to hear what her Mom said, but upon further thought, she knew that wasn't the way to go. So, she got up and went downstairs and sat down at the table.

"Thank you for coming down. I need to apologize for how I acted the other day. You were right. No matter my reasoning, I should not have lied to you. You see...my Dad, your grandfather ran out on me and my Mom. I was so caught up on what he did to me that I wasn't even thinking about you. I thought I was keeping you safe by not talking about him or telling you about him so that way he wouldn't be in a position to let you down too. But after our talk, I did some serious thinking and I realized that I was actually trying to protect myself. I didn't want to see him again. I didn't want him to be a part of my life and I didn't stop to think about if you want him in your life. Obviously, you have taken a liking to him and he *has* helped you with your power so maybe as much as I don't want to admit it...he's changed. And so far, he has been consistent. So, I promise you that I won't let my anger get in the way of us again. We are a team. We always have been and you are right. Lying is wrong no matter how you frame it. But you will see as you get older, the line between right and wrong gets blurry. I hope your friends can help you when you face a situation like this one and set you straight like how you helped me. Now, can I have a hug from my daughter?" Ms. Monroe asked as she reached out her arms.

"Yes," Diana said as she embraced Ms. Monroe.

The hug lasted what felt like hours but when it was over.

"Okay, now let's eat before it gets cold," Ms. Monroe said as she started fixing their plates.

"Umm, there's one more thing I found out at Tyson's," Diana started to say.

"What did you find?"

"Well, we were confused about it, but it said *active* next to Vendetta's name on the website we used," Diana said.

"Well, what website was it?" Ms. Monroe asked.

"Tyson's uncle works for the government and he may or may not let us use his computer," Diana said with a wide smile.

"You stole a laptop and you were upset about me lying.... Diana?!" Ms. Monroe asked.

"No, no we didn't steal his laptop. We told him that we were suspicious about Vendetta being related to me and we asked him to use it. He didn't exactly say yes but that was because he didn't want to risk his job. So, he just told us where it was and told us not to get him fired," Diana explained.

"I don't want him watching you all anymore but about the active thing. I'll ask Vendetta about it later," Ms. Monroe said.

"Moooommm. His uncle is cool and he probably didn't think we would find anything. He wouldn't have let us use the laptop if there was a way we would find something we shouldn't see. We're just kids," Diana said.

"Okay, okay I can understand how he underestimated you all but I'm still going to have a talk with him," Ms. Monroe said.

"Fair enough. There's one more thing I have to tell you," Diana said.

"Okay. Hit me," Ms. Monroe said.

"There's one more person who knows or thinks they know about my power," Diana said with a wide smile.

"Who is it? And why didn't you tell me? I thought you were mad at me for lying," Ms. Monroe said.

"Her name is Hannah. She's on the debate team with me, but I think we've come to an understanding. I still don't actually know if she knows or not or just thinks I'm weird. I wanted to be sure before I told you but because we had this talk I figured I should just tell you now," Diana explained.

"Unnhuhh. Okay. I forgive you for not telling me and you forgive me too right?" Ms. Monroe asked.

"Of course. Water under the bridge. Pish posh," Diana assured Ms. Monroe.

"Well this is enough honesty for one day," Ms. Monroe said with a chuckle.

"Yea, that was a lot," Diana said.

"How is your team speech coming along for the competition," Ms. Monroe asked.

"Good considering my partner is Hannah, but I'm excited. I really want to win. I've been practicing my part of the speech every night, practicing saying it out loud and memorizing it well enough so hopefully, I won't mess up. I don't have much time left since the competition is around the corner," Diana said.

"I know. I've been hearing it every night," Ms. Monroe said with a chuckle.

"Sorry, I just want to be prepared," Diana said.

"Don't apologize. I like how dedicated you are. It doesn't keep me up at all or bother me. I just heard you practice so much I wanted to know how it was going," Ms. Monroe explained.

"I really like it. It's fun to argue….in an acceptable way of course," Diana said with a chuckle.

"Riiiight. Well, I'm excited to watch you do your thing and tell everyone you're my little girl," Ms. Monroe said.

"Mooomm, I'm in the sixth grade," Diana insisted.

"I know, I know. But you will always be my little girl, even when you're thirty years old," Ms. Monroe said.

It was the next day and Diana was getting ready for school. She knew Steph and Tyson would be curious about what happened and she wanted to confront Mr. Vendetta. However, she had to put those thoughts out of her head because she was expected to meet with the debate team before school and she needed her head clear and focused.

When Diana arrived at school, the sky was still dark but she saw other cars in the drop-off lane. She was excited about the meet-up, she'd never been this early to school before. She could see Mr. Kyle standing near the entrance doors, holding them open for the other team members. After they had entered and gathered in the cafeteria Mr. Kyle started his speech.

"I wanted you all to come early today to give you a feel for how tomorrow will go. I wanted you to see how it feels to wake up this early and so that you could work out any kinks like differences in traffic, breakfast, and things like that before the competition tomorrow. Hopefully, things will go smoothly. It looks like all of you are here so that is great. Do any of you have any questions?" Mr. Kyle asked.

"Will we have to bring our own lunches tomorrow?" Stacy asked.

"No, there are refreshments and lunches for the students," Hannah answered.

"Thank you, Hannah," Mr. Kyle said.

"I will go over the itinerary. First, we will board the bus at 7:00 am. Then, we will get to the center at 9:00 am. Once we get there we will be shown our preparation rooms and there will be an opening/welcome speech in the auditorium. Then at 10:30 am, the competition will start. I've printed out the schedule of the actual competition for your teams and will give them to you on the bus tomorrow. There will be an intermission for lunch at 11:30 am and the competition will start up again at 12:30 pm. The trophy ceremony will be at 2:00 pm. Then, we will get ready to leave around 2:45 pm to get back to the school at 5:00 pm. Are there any questions?" Mr. Kyle asked. He was met with silence.

"I will take that as a no. I also want to take the time out to thank you all for your hard work. You don't know how much your dedication means to me, as your mentor. Regardless of what happens tomorrow, I am proud of every single one of you. Let's do our best tomorrow!" Mr. Kyle exclaimed.

"Yeah!" the students respond, raising their fists in the air.

"Since you all have about 45 minutes before classes start, use your time wisely and maybe go over your speech with your partner," Mr. Kyle said. All the members started to converse with their partners as Mr. Kyle suggested.

"So, Hannah, do you want to practice our speech?" Diana asked.

"Yeah, we can. Have you memorized everything? The judges don't like it if you have to look at your cheat cards. Memorizing is more impressive," Hannah said.

"I did. I know everything by heart now," Diana said.

"Okay, let's try this out," Hannah said.

The girls practiced their speeches for about 40 minutes.

"Now, remember, you are my defense. You have to have my back in this. I know we don't really have a relationship like that, but we have to be professional about this," Hannah said.

"I have your back for the competition," Diana responded.

"Alright, and don't get too upset again like you did last time we debated," Hannah said.

"That was different. We weren't on the same side," Diana said.

"I know, but if you feel as strongly as you do about global warming as you do about sharks then just watch your *weirdness* okay. Your friends won't be able to be there to help you this time," Hannah said.

"I have everything under control. I'll be fine," Diana said.

"You better because I don't lose. It's almost time for class. See you tomorrow," Hannah said.

"Uh Huh...see ya," Diana said, a bit confused.

Everyone started to head to class. Diana knew she didn't have enough time to find Mr. Vendetta and confront him. So, she decided to find him during lunch. When she arrived at class, Steph and Tyson were clearly worried by the obvious concern in their eyes, but were relieved when Diana gave them a big hug and told them she had worked it out with her Mom.

"That's great. I knew everything would work out!" Steph said as she gave Diana yet another hug.

"Have you talked to Mr. Vendetta?" Tyson asked.

"I haven't, actually. I'm going to skip lunch and talk to him then," Diana said.

"Well, we are here for you, Diana, if you need us," Tyson said.

"I know. I have the best friends in the world," Diana said.

"Alright class, please take your seats. We will be reviewing today and ending class with playing Kahoot!" Mr. Campbell said.

"Yess!" the class said in unison as they all started to sit down.

Later, when it was time for the class to head to lunch, Diana told Mr. Campbell that she had to go to the restroom and was excused. The first place Diana checked was his office and he wasn't there. So, she started to walk the halls and hoped she saw him. She almost gave up until she made that final turn, in the hallway toward the cafeteria, and saw him walking into a classroom. So, she headed in the same direction.

"Hey, *Mr. Vendetta*," Diana said as she entered the room.

"Hello, Diana. Shouldn't you be at lunch?" Mr. Vendetta asked, confused as to why she said his name like that.

"You've been lying to me. Why didn't you tell me you were my grandfather?" Diana asked angrily.

I knew you'd find out eventually…. It's complicated," Mr. Vendetta started to say.

"I know. I know how my Mom feels about you and the gist of what happened," Diana said.

"Well, then you know that I left her…your Mother, and her Mom a long time ago," Mr. Vendetta said.

"Why did you leave?" Diana asked.

"It's complicated," Mr. Vendetta said.

"Why is everything so complicated? Did you not love them?" Diana asked with tears brimming her eyes.

"Of course, I love them. You don't know…. I can't tell you what happened. You will have to trust that it was for a good reason," Mr. Vendetta said, trying to hold back tears.

"How can I trust you again if you won't tell me? Are you going to leave me too for some reason you won't be able to tell me?" Diana asked.

"You have trusted me this whole time and I haven't done you any harm," Mr. Vendetta said while holding Diana's hands and looking her in the eyes.

"Please, I promise you there is a good reason. Allow me to continue to help you and earn your trust back. I just want a relationship with you...that is if you'd be okay with that," Mr. Vendetta said.

"I can't exactly argue with you on that...Can I call you Grandpa now?" Diana asked shyly.

"Umm not at school but I'd love that, Diana," Mr. Vendetta said with a smile.

"Deal," Diana said, as she gave him a hug.

"Okay, you need to head back to class. If you can get to my office, there's an apple in there since you missed your lunch," Mr. Vendetta said.

"Okay...oh are you still going to be able to sneak on the bus tomorrow for the competition?" Diana asked excitedly.

"Of, course. How could I ever miss my dear granddaughter's competition that she's been working so hard for. Now go before you're late," Mr. Vendetta said with a smile while waving her goodbye.

Diana was still able to get to Mr. Vendetta's office and got the apple and took a few bites before class officially started. Steph and Tyson let out a sigh of relief when Diana came in with an apple in her hand and not looking upset. However, they weren't able to talk to her until it was time to play Kahoot.

"So how did it go? Good right, you don't look upset," Steph inferred.

"Yeah it went pretty good. I'm still upset that he didn't tell me and that he left my Mom and his wife for a reason that he also can't tell me. However, I have decided to trust him until he has given me a reason not to. I do have to say it's nice having a grandad. I can actually call him that now," Diana explained.

"More family is always good. I'm happy for you," Steph said.

"I'm happy for you too. At least you all have a clean slate now being that everyone knows everything," Tyson said.

"Yeah, that's true," Diana said.

Realization

"Well, I don't know about y'all but I'm about to win this game," Steph said with a smirk.

"I'm the master of Kahoot. No one will beat Tyson106," Tyson said confidently.

"Tyson106? Really? That's what you came up with?" Diana asked.

"Heyyy, I like my username and it's never failed me. At least mine isn't boring like just my name," Tyson retorted.

"Your name is literally half your actual name with three numbers at the end," Steph said.

"It's still better than yours. You'll see when I pummel you in this game,"

"Okay, Tyson106. We'll see about that," Steph said as they all proceeded to play the game.

Toward the end of class...

"So, are you excited about your competition tomorrow?" Tyson asked.

"Oh, so you're trying to change the subject since you lost, huh?" Diana asked.

"Boring ole Steph won and Tyson106 got *second* place," Steph said, taunting him.

"Okay, okay. You beat me. I'll get you next time," Tyson assures them.

"I'll believe it when I see it," Diana said.

"But, seriously, how are you feeling about tomorrow?" Tyson asked.

"I'm excited. I feel as prepared as I'll ever be. Hannah is also prepared. I think we'll kill it," Diana said.

"That's the attitude. I can't wait to go to the dinner and hear all about it," Steph said.

"I am too. Red Lobster is my favorite restaurant," Diana said.

"I've never been, but I heard they have great biscuits. I'm excited to try those…and of course, hear how great you did, Diana," Tyson said.

"Oh, yes. You definitely aren't going just because of their biscuits. You're really something else. You know that?" Diana asked.

"I try, I try," Tyson replies.

Ding Ding

"Alright class. Have a great rest of your day and those of you on the debate team, I wish you all the best of luck tomorrow," Mr. Campbell said.

"Well, see you guys tomorrow, "Diana said as she gave Steph and Tyson a hug.

"Bye!" Tyson and Steph responded as they hugged her back.

Diana proceeded to walk to the car-rider area. She could see Ms. Monroe's car in the line. "This time tomorrow, I'll be a winner of my very first debating competition," Diana thought to herself. When she got in the car, sleep came over Diana. Right when they arrived home Diana woke up and Ms. Monroe started to prepare dinner. She was making her famous spaghetti.

Diana was excited but she was also very nervous. She has been putting up a confident face in front of her friends, but on the inside, she is afraid that she may not be prepared enough, that she isn't truly cut out for this, that she will lose. Instead of dwelling on her thoughts, she decided to keep herself busy and do some dot-to-dot to pass time until dinner was ready.

"Dinner's ready," Ms. Monroe said.

"Coming," Diana said as she came down the stairs.

"Set the table for me, please," Ms. Monroe asked.

"Okay," Diana said as she put the plates, forks, and napkins on the table.

"Now, before we eat, I want you to listen to me. You were asleep in the car and I didn't want to disturb you, but I'm your Mom and I know how you are. I raised you to be confident and you are, but you tend to doubt yourself. I want you to know that I believe in you and I know you will do great tomorrow and I'm not just saying that because I'm your Mom, I really mean it. I've heard you night after night reciting your speech and perfecting it, I almost know it. You don't need to worry. No matter what happens tomorrow, find comfort in that you have done everything you could possibly do, your absolute best," Ms. Monroe said.

"Thanks, Mom. I needed that," Diana said.

"You're welcome. Moms have powers too you know. We know when there's something bothering our babies," Ms. Monroe claimed.

"I know, I know," Diana agreed as she gave her Mom a hug.

"Now let's eat, because I'm hungry," Ms. Monroe said.

"You don't have to tell me twice," Diana said as she began fixing her plate.

Later that night, Diana decided to meditate with her Mom to clear her head and center herself for the competition tomorrow. Afterward, with a clear mind, she was able to sleep soundly.

The next morning Diana woke up to her alarm and started to get ready for the competition immediately. Ms. Monroe had her clothes ironed for her and hung on her door. Diana could smell her Mom cooking what smelt like bacon and eggs. When she got downstairs, Ms. Monroe was already dressed and setting the table with a huge smile on her face.

"Today's the day! I have eggs, bacon, and toast. I didn't want to make too much and have all of that sitting on your stomach for your debate," Ms. Monroe.

"Thanks, Mom. I'm happy you were able to be off work to watch me, Mr. Vendetta is coming too," Diana said.

"Well, you know I wouldn't miss this for the world. I love you so much," Ms. Monroe said as she gave her a huge kiss on her forehead.

"Mooommm," Diana complained as she wiped her forehead.

"Heyy, don't wipe away my kiss," Ms. Monroe jokingly said.

After they ate breakfast, they got in the car and headed for the school. When they pulled up. They saw a huge blue and white bus. "Things are starting to get real," Diana thought to herself. They could see there were a few people already on the bus. Ms. Monroe has packed them both a neck pillow and blanket in case the bus was cold or if they wanted to take a nap until they arrived.

As they walked to the bus, Diana started to look for Mr. Vendetta, but he wasn't anywhere to be seen. She didn't think anything of it since it was still pretty early. However, as time passed and more and more people showed up, Diana started to worry he wouldn't make it. Ms. Monroe noticed Diana's concern.

Realization

"He'll be here. If he said he will be here then we will. He hasn't given you a reason to doubt him yet, has he?" she asked.

"No, he hasn't," Diana replied.

It was ten minutes until the bus was supposed to pull off and Mr. Vendetta still hadn't shown up. This time, Ms. Monroe was not giving encouraging words, she was in fact starting to get angry. Then, at the last call, Mr. Vendetta stepped onto the bus in a grey and white suit, shocking Diana and Ms. Monroe. Diana had never seen Ms. Vendetta dressed up in anything other than his school uniform.

"I'm sorry I'm so late, I had to find my tie," Mr. Vendetta said as he sat across from them.

"I'm just happy you're here," Diana said, feeling relieved.

"How could I miss my granddaughter's competition," Mr. Vendetta assured.

Then the doors of the bus closed and the bus started to drive off. The drive felt longer than it actually was. The neck pillows and blanket came in handy when both Diana and Ms. Monroe decided to take a nap halfway through the ride. When they arrived, Mr. Kyle woke everyone up and went over the itinerary one more time, and instructed them to leave their personal items on the bus and enter the building and wait for their guide to their room.

At the entrance, there was a woman waiting for them and escorted them to their room. It was a large circular room with many chairs and two podiums so they could practice their speeches if they wanted to. All the parents and other guests besides the children were sent to another room, most likely the auditorium.

"You ready for this?" Hannah asked, startling Diana a bit.

"Oh, yeah," Diana assured her.

"Alright you better because I want to win," Hannah said.

"So, do I," Diana agreed.

"Great, then we have an understanding and a common enemy," Hannah said.

Realization

"Okay, children, will you please follow me to the auditorium for the welcoming speech?" their escort said.

The children followed her lead and walked to the auditorium. There were many kids from other schools and at least 200 guests in the back. So, naturally, Diana scanned the room for her Mom and Mr. Vendetta. She found them towards the upper corner and waved at them before she sat down. The welcoming speech was very long-winded and almost put everyone to sleep, but that did not dull Diana's excitement for the competition. After it was over, the kids were escorted back to their rooms so the competition could officially begin.

To pass the time, Diana practiced her speech a few more times and conversed with some of the other members. When it came time to eat, Diana was interested in what kind of fancy lunches they had prepared for them. To her surprise, it was a mere sandwich, apple, and bag of chips. "This is worse than the school lunch," Diana thought to herself. However, she ate it anyway and was grateful because she was always taught to be grateful for food because while she may not consider the food to be high quality there could be people out in the world who have no food at all.

After lunch, the competition started again and Diana was starting to get anxious and even started to sweat. She didn't want her nerves to get the best of her so she decided to find a spot near the back of the room to meditate. She had just started to close her eyes and tune out all the other noise in the room when Hannah approached her.

"What are you doing? Sleeping?" Hannah asked.

"No, I'm *trying* to meditate to calm my nerves," Diana said.

"You're weird," Hannah said.

"And you're interrupting me. So, if you have nothing helpful to say please leave me alone," Diana said with a snarky smile.

"Fine, weirdo. You better be ready when it's time for us to go," Hannah said.

"I will," Diana said confidently.

Diana started focusing on her breathing and all the different parts of her body, imagining slowing everything down. She envisioned herself laying in her room on her bed, listening to jungle sounds in the dark, looking up at the stars on her ceiling, and the world stopped for a moment. Diana stayed like this for about twenty minutes and when she stopped she felt very relaxed and ready for the competition.

It was finally time for Diana and Hannah to go up to the stage to compete. The escort showed them to the back entrance to the auditorium and the show was getting ready to begin.

"Hannah and Diana from the Pedita Middle School please come on stage," the host instructed as the girls walked onto the stage.

"This group will be debating for there to be measures put in place to prevent further global warming. Whereas Jason and Rebecca from Lively Middle School will be the opposition. Pedita Middle School will start," the host said as he gestured for Hannah to walk up to the platform.

Excerpt from Hannah's argument

Global warming is a serious problem in the world. The effects of this will impact everyone and individuals who have not even been born yet. So, why are there little to no measures in place to prevent further global warming? It is safe to assume that most of the people in this very room were transported here by a vehicle that burns fossil fuels. Yes, it is convenient, but it is causing carbon dioxide to be released into our earth's atmosphere and it is getting trapped. This is causing the earth to heat up. This will lead to intense droughts, deathly hurricanes, the melting of icebergs, heat waves, the rising of sea levels, extinction of marine species near coral reefs, more allergies, and deadly diseases in humans. The major companies that we rely on have known that their harmful emissions would cause problems. It was told to them by the scientist they hired and they chose to do nothing. Because of this, now we are seeing the effects in the melting of the polar ice caps, the rising of sea levels, and heat waves just as predicted. Will we have to wait until people start to lose their lives from the effects of global warming before policies are put in place to combat it? I stand that we should not...

Excerpt from Jason's rebuttal

Are we even sure that climate change truly exists to the degree at which certain scientists have said? Hasn't the earth's climate fluctuated since the beginning of its existence? Could this fluctuation not be a natural occurrence? How are we so sure that it was the cause of these emissions that truly affect the high variables in the atmosphere and not some other underlying issue that scientists are unaware of? All scientists cannot even agree as to global warming's existence, so why should we spend billions of dollars to combat it, because that's how much it would take for the appropriate measures to be put in place to combat something that may or may not exist, just because some scientists believe in it, or a prediction. Scientists can't properly predict a mere earthquake, but they are so certain that they can predict the end of life as we know it with the occurrence of hurricanes, droughts, allergies, and diseases. Is that what we are supposed to believe? Oftentimes meteorologists' predictions of the weather are wrong. I can expect that most of you here have had those days where snow was predicted that never came or rain that never fell. We cannot afford to spend billions of dollars and completely change our way of life for a mere prediction. That is why I don't believe there should be measures put in place to prevent this approximation...

Excerpt from Diana's argument

Not only do ninety-nine percent of scientists agree that climate change is real and affecting us at an alarming rate, but they also agree that humans are the reason for it. Meaning it is not simply a natural occurrence in the earth. The rising levels of heat on this planet is at a rate never seen before in earth's history. Yes, it takes substantial funds to reduce humans' carbon footprint, but it doesn't take much to start. One easy way to reduce our carbon footprint is to start car-pooling to get to places so fewer emissions are being released and trapped in the atmosphere. Another way is to eat food that can normally be grown in your area to reduce the emission released by the travel of exported foods. Another way is to change your regular light bulbs to LED light bulbs which use a quarter of the energy and last up to 25 times longer. One more would be to keep your tires in your car inflated and remove extra weight from the car which would increase the fuel efficiency. Not only could the common person utilize these tips in their daily life, but these changes don't just benefit the environment but our daily life as well; such as not needing to buy more bulbs as often, saving money on gas with car-pooling, and having fewer issues with our cars due to the increased efficiency. We live in a closed system, whatever we do here on earth will affect us in the long run because we can't escape the atmosphere. Have any of you ever thought about where your trash goes after the trashmen pick it up? It doesn't just go away, they can't send it out in space either. Trash won't decompose like flesh, it will sit there. And while, yes, it is grinded up, we *cannot effectively get rid of it. The trash from 200 years ago is still here on this earth and just like trash, harmful emissions of CO_2 are being trapped here as well as causing problems for the human race. Soon we'll be caught in hurricanes like Hurricane Katrina that was presumed to only be a category three but was responsible for thousands of people being injured and several hundred dead. Are we going to wait until these huge, destructive storms start to happen even more than they already are? Hundreds of people on average will die if nothing is done about climate change. That is not a prediction, but a scary fact. This does not include the average death toll per year which is around 45 million across the world which will increase with various heat waves causing droughts which lead to dehydration that will surely increase if no policies are put in place now. I ask again how many people have to die for there to be policies brought into place to stop this human-induced disaster that is global warming...*

Excerpt from Rebecca's rebuttal

Implementing protocol would most certainly prove extremely challenging for the human race. There is a huge issue of income inequality in most parts of the world. Where are they going to get the money for these more expensive LED bulbs? Where are people going to find the money to pay to ensure their car is in tiptop condition? Most Americans, in general, can't afford health insurance for illnesses/diseases/injuries they already have and you expect them to spend their hard-earned money to implement these measures that could possibly prevent illnesses no one has yet? Let's think realistically here, you expect people to not even purchase items that have to be sent overseas. So, no more fruits and vegetables if they don't grow in your country, no more comfy furniture for your house, no more cars, no more cell phones, no more televisions, no more clothes to wear, and no more toys for your children if they cannot be made in your own country. That is absolutely too much to give up for mere prediction. Might I also mention that those are just the most popular items that are commonly shipped overseas. There would be more that would have to go if global warming measures were put in place. The huge companies that are supposedly emitting the most carbon in the atmosphere are the same ones that allow us to have gas and transportation that brought us here today to this competition. So, should they be negatively impacted, having to change to renewable resources which means rendering the cars that people already acquire to be useless? Does everyone have the income to afford a Tesla? No, they don't and they shouldn't be worried about losing their livelihood. Global warming, if it is truly real, measures should, therefore, not be put in place...

"This concludes the global warming debate. Contestants, please exit the stage and the winning team will be announced during the award ceremony. Thank you," The host stated.

Hannah and Diana walked back to their room. Diana was highly upset about the other team's argument.

"How could they do that? How could they disregard the lives that could be affected? How can they use those extreme measures that really don't have to take place to justify their argument?" Diana asked while steaming.

"They were doing their job. They were putting up a good compelling argument and just because they said it doesn't mean they believe it, themselves. It wasn't their choice to get the opposing argument. They had to work with what they had just like we did," Hannah explained.

"Okay, I get that. But do you really think the judges are going to pick their side over ours? I mean all they could talk about is that it would impact people's livelihood. Shouldn't people care about our human race as a whole? Shouldn't we be trying to do everything we can to prevent deaths and diseases even if that means making a few uncomfortable changes?" Diana asked.

"You're so young," Hannah said.

"You are literally one year older than me," Diana said.

"Well, when you're older you will realize that people care way more about themselves than they do about other people. People act in their own self-interest," Hannah says.

"But a lot of people give back to the community, hold fundraisers for charity, and doctors and nurses help sick people and they don't get anything from that," Diana said.

"They do, actually. They get the satisfaction that they did the *right* thing for someone who is in a bad situation. However, not all people care to feel that kind of satisfaction. That's just the way the world works. There are some people who are like you, who like to help people and look out for others, but as you get older that number dwindles and people become more selfish. Of course, that is not the case for every single person but, it is true for most, sadly," Hannah said.

Realization

"Well, I hope the judges are people that agree with me, that saving lives is more important and worth having to change a few aspects of our livelihood," Dian said.

"I do too because that would mean we won. We will be the winners," Hannah said.

"Yeah, of course, that too," Diana said.

When they reached their room, they were pestered with questions by the other teammates like, "How did it go? How do you think you did? Were there a lot of people watching? How did the judges look while you spoke?" After answering their questions, Diana went back to the back of the room and waited. After about thirty more minutes the awards ceremony was about to begin and Diana was basically shaking, anticipating the results.

They were gathered back in the auditorium and the winners were called on stage to be given shiny gold medals. The other team would be given a participation trophy. They were announcing them based on the groups that went first so Diana knew she'd be called towards the end. While she waited, she looked up at Mr. Vendetta and Ms. Monroe. They both gave her an encouraging thumbs-up and bright smile. Then, it was finally time to hear the results from Diana's group.

"The winner for the global warming debate is...Team Jason and Rebecca from Lively Middle School! Come up and receive your medal!"

Diana's chest began to tighten as she kept the tears at bay while clapping for the other team. She worked so hard on her speech and she wasn't able to convince the judges. What was she going to tell Steph and Tyson? What is the reason for having a celebratory dinner for a loser? Those questions filled Diana's mind as she and Hannah walked up to the other side of the stage to receive their participation trophy. While Diana was up there she was surprised at Ms. Monroe and Mr. Vendetta cheering and standing up in the crowd. "Did they not get what I lost?" Diana thought to herself.

After the award ceremony, the kids were free to go greet their guests before it was time to get back to the buses. Diana had a solemn look on her face when Ms. Monroe and Mr. Vendetta saw her walking toward them.

"She must be devastated. Let me talk to her," Ms. Monroe said.

"If it's okay, I think I can handle this one," Mr. Vendetta said.

"Okay, go ahead. I'll be waiting by the bus," Ms. Monroe said.

"Hey, why the sad face? You looked great out there," Mr. Vendetta asked.

"But I didn't win," Diana said.

"Now, you know that everything is not about winning," Mr. Vendetta said.

"It doesn't change the fact that I lost and it sucks," Diana said.

"Yes, losing isn't pleasant to say the least. However, it does present you with a great opportunity," Mr. Vendetta said.

"And what could that be?" Diana said.

"A chance for you to determine who you are by your actions. After losing there are only two options. Let this stop you from pursuing something you truly enjoy and have worked so tirelessly for and give up, *or* to decide to keep trying and getting better so you lessen your chances of losing ever again. Many people try and fail, but many people are not strong or determined enough to fail until they win. Who will you be?" Mr. Vendetta asked.

"I... will be the weak person that gives up," Diana said.

"Diaannaaaaa," Mr. Vendetta said,

"Okay, okay, I'll be strong," Diana said.

"That's my girl," Mr. Vendetta said.

"See, why can't I be good at changing peoples' minds and convincing them like you just did to me?" Diana said.

"You will not always be able to change someone's mind or convince them to believe in something you do or even like what you like and that shouldn't be your goal," Mr. Vendetta said.

"That is the whole point of debating, providing a convincing argument," Diana said.

"While that may be the case, that is only the case for debating but not in everyday life. The most important thing is believing in what you wish to believe in, doing what makes you happy, and liking yourself for who you are. Don't you like who you are?" Mr. Vendetta asked.

"Well, yes, but Hannah said that there are a lot of people out there who don't think the way I do or care like I care and it was because of that, that we lost against the other team. The way I think literally puts me on the losing team," Diana said.

"I'll put it this way. Do you like ketchup?" Mr. Vendetta asked.

Yes, I love ketchup," Diana said.

"Well, I don't like ketchup. It's terrible. I would never eat any a day in my life. Does that change your view of ketchup?" Mr. Vendetta asked.

"No, I still love ketchup. I put it on everything," Diana said.

"That is the attitude you should have when it comes to other things in life that you are passionate about. See. everyone has different sauces and people may not like your sauce but what's most important is..." Mr. Vendetta said, motioning for Diana to finish it.

"If I like my sauce?" Diana said.

"Yes, exactly. The same way you like ketchup and I don't is the same way people could disagree with your argument, but you shouldn't work yourself up over it, because the only thing that matters is that you did your best and that you are proud of your arguments."

"But, the whole competition is based on if the judges like my sauce more than someone else's. That's the only way I win. How can I not get upset about it if they don't like my sauce? Why are we talking about sauces anyways?" Diana asked.

"You have to accept the fact that those people are going to feel the way they are going to feel about your argument. Your passion for your *sauce* is not going to influence them any more than your original speech. You will never be able to force someone to agree with you and that's okay. You cannot depend on others' approval. You cannot tie your happiness to their opinion on your sauce, because if you do then you would be handicapping yourself. You are going to give them all you've got and they will make the decision. If it doesn't go your way, it is certainly okay to feel disappointed, but it wouldn't be okay for it to change the way you view your sauce. You should still be proud of yourself and try again and most importantly, still be happy you gave it your all. Okay?" Mr. Vendetta explained.

"Okayyyy," Diana said.

"Good. Now I don't know about you but I would like to get to Red Lobster so I can celebrate my granddaughter participating in her first debate competition and killing it," Mr. Vendetta said as he started walking toward the bus.

"I'm coming. I'm coming. I am looking forward to the garlic shrimp," Diana said with a smile.

Realization

"There's that smile. Your Mom is waiting for you on the bus, be warned she plans on hugging and kissing you until you smile. So, keep that smile on your face if you don't want pink lipstick all over it," Mr. Vendetta said as they walked toward the bus.

"Thanks for the warning," Diana said as she ran ahead to the bus.

Mr. Vendetta was right, as soon as Diana made it to the bus, the kissing and hugging started. "I'm seriously starting to second guess inviting my Mom to another one of these ever again," she joked to herself. On the ride back to the school, Diana and Ms. Monroe fell asleep, yet again and woke up to the sound of everyone departing from the bus. It was about 5:30 pm when they arrived and the reservations were at 6:30 pm. So, they quickly put their neck pillows and blankets in the car and pulled off with Mr. Vendetta following closely behind.

They arrived at the restaurant in the nick of time. Luckily, Tyson, Stephanie, and her parents were already there so they could go ahead and get seated. After Ms. Monroe announced that Diana's team didn't win but did an amazing job they all still had a huge smile on their faces and proceeded to hug Diana until she could barely breathe.

"I'm so proud of you for doing it!!" Steph said.

"Me too, I can't wait to see the video your Mom recorded," Tyson said.

"Aww, thanks guys but I'm hungry so let's go ahead and order," Diana said and the table filled with laughter.

"Hello everyone, what can I get you all today?" the waitress asked

As everyone started to order, Tyson was busy filling his face with biscuits.

"You like them huh?" Diana asked Tyson.

"Oh yes. Oh, this- This right here. I'm in love. I don't want anything else, I just want a couple more baskets of bread," Tyson said.

"Come on, you have to order *something* else. This is a seafood restaurant, not a bread restaurant," Steph insisted.

"I don't care, it's too good, nothing can compare," Tyson said.

"I agree with him," Steph's Dad said.

"Daadd," Steph said.

"What he's not wrong. They are awesome but you really should order something else. I recommend the crab legs," Steph's Dad said.

"Okay, I'll try it since you suggested it," Tyson said.

"Really, you listen to him and not me?" Steph said.

"Yes," Tyson responded with a shrug.

"Wooooww," Steph said.

Diana was busy trying to help her Mom decide what she wanted to eat and Mr. Vendetta gets a phone call.

"Excuse me for a second, I need to go take this," Mr. Vendetta said nervously.

"Do you think everything's okay?" Steph whispered to Tyson.

"I'm sure everything is fine. It's not like he's informing the government that Diana didn't use her powers at the competition to win," Tyson said with a chuckle.

"I'm not having a good feeling about this. What if…what if he is working for them and just watching Diana for them?" Steph said.

"Normally your gut feeling is really good, but this is way off. Why would he tell the government about Diana in the first place when he knows firsthand how he was probably treated by them?" Tyson asked.

"Wait, what do you mean by him experiencing it firsthand?" Steph asked.

"I mean he has the power. So, that is probably why he was in the government system at some point and why his name was changed and stuff. So, why would he rat Diana out?"

"He has the power too? Are you serious? You knew this whole time and didn't feel like informing us? Your friends?"

"What do you mean? We've been over this. That's why I was so sleepy cause I was keeping it from you until Mr. Vendetta told y'all himself. I thought he told you that day you said everything was fine between us," Tyson said.

"That's not what he said," Steph said angrily.

"Hello? Why are you calling me?" Mr. Vendetta asked.

Realization

"Is that any way to talk to your old friend who has always looked out for you?"

"You are not, have not been, and will never be my friend. Now, what do you want, Todd?" Mr. Vendetta asked.

"I want to know how Diana handled the loss in the competition," Todd said.

"Why? She is none of your concern," Mr. Vendetta asked.

"Oh yes, she is and you know it," Todd said,

"I don't know what you're alluding to but you're wrong," Mr. Vendetta.

"I don't think I am. I know she has the power. You thought you could just change your name and move across a couple of states and think we wouldn't find you and keep tabs on you. You're smarter than that," Todd said,

"How did you find out? Who told you?"

"I placed my daughter in her school and instructed her to piss her off to see if she has it and that brat does everything I tell her to," Todd explained.

"And you're the reason they lost the competition?" Mr. Vendetta said angrily.

"I called in a favor," Todd said.

"You had no right to do that and you have no claim to my granddaughter," Mr. Vendetta said.

"I will do as I please and I will be in touch to tell you how things are going to go from now on and if you don't comply then you know what will happen," Todd said.

"I'm okay with that," Mr. Vendetta said nervously.

"But are you okay with it happening to Diana...I thought so," Todd said.

Call ended.

The End

ABOUT THE AUTHOR

Hello, everyone! My name is Emani Sawyer and this is the story of how I began to write this book. I had wanted to write this book since the Fall of 2015. However, I didn't because I felt like I wasn't the typical writer. I don't find myself writing to calm me or something that brings me an overwhelming sense of joy, but this story was on my heart. In the end, I decided to keep this story in the vault and left it alone. Then in Fall 2016, my life changed forever. I went to the doctor's office for a regular check-up that led to 4 heart surgeries. When I arrived, I was asked if I wouldn't mind seeing a new doctor who had just come back from having breast cancer and I said sure, I don't mind. After listening to my heart, she had a perplexing look on her face and suggested I go to a cardiac specialist. She assured me that it was probably nothing major, in the hopes of not wanting me to panic because, as we later found out, she knew what was happening all along.

About the Author

When I had my appointment at the specialist office I found out that I had a whole in the septum of my heart. I was called an Atrial Septal Defect. To put it in simple terms, I had a whole in the wall that separated my right ventricle from the left, causing my oxygenated blood to mix with my de-oxygenated blood and that I had it since I was born. Growing up, I was told I had asthma and was given an asthma pump that was supposed to help with the pain and shortness of breath I would feel after physical activity. However, the opposite occurred after taking the pump, I would feel worse... So, I decided to stop taking it and just tough it out. Throughout my childhood I participated in many extracurricular activities such as dance, gymnastics, and Taekwondo. My specialist as well as the other doctors who ended up hearing about my defect were shocked that I was still alive, being that I was supposed to have surgery to fix this while at four-five months old and I lasted fifteen years, while participating in those activities. After this revelation, I was told I needed to have surgery to fix it. First, they tried to do a minimal invasive surgery, but it was unsuccessful due to the size of the material they had used to try and patch the whole. So, I went under again, this time with the biggest piece of material they had and it was still too small and while they were in there they were able to see that the right side of my heart was enlarged and that blood had been flowing into my lungs. So, open heart surgery was my only option at that point. In a matter of three days they flew in practitioners from across state lines to be my team to get the surgery done as soon as possible, being that my life depended on it. They had planned to use pig skin as a substitute for my wall in order to patch the whole. That was a risky move since my body could easily reject it, making matters a lot worse, but they had to try. Believe it or not I wasn't scared. I knew I had to have had God on my side because he kept me here on this earth even when science deemed it to be practically impossible and I knew if he pulled me through this surgery I was meant to do something of value, something meaningful. When they conducted the surgery, they found a sort of flap of skin, the perfect size of the whole, where the wall should have been and the surgeon was able to unfold it and patch up the whole without needing the pig skin, another blessing from the Lord. After the surgery I was recovering well. I was left with a beautiful scar that has become a symbol for me to admire all that I had overcome to be where I am now. Then, after four months I had to fight for my life yet again. I'm not the person to cry when I'm in pain. So, my mother knew if I was crying then I needed to go to the hospital, given my high pain tolerance. When I got into a room and was checked they told me I needed to have emergency heart surgery again, right away or I would die. I needed a pericardial effusion, in plain terms; since my heart had been cut open in order to patch the

About the Author

whole, my body thought it would be a great idea to send fluid to the area, but the fluid never subsided, it kept building and building. As this was happening the outer walls of my heart were growing bigger, swollen, virtually drowning and suffocating my heart at the same time, not allowing it to function properly. Luckily, I had gotten to the hospital in enough time and was able to have the surgery to release the fluid. However, the swelling wouldn't go down, causing me to have to take steroids in order to stop the swelling, but it resulted in me gaining around 75 pounds in only three and a half months. However, despite that I was happy to be alive and more determined than ever to figure out what I was meant to do in this world. After all, I couldn't have cheated death twice and not have something meant for me to do and it dawned on me, my book. I was stuck on the fact that I wasn't the stereotypical writer-type, but that didn't block me anymore. I knew this book that you have just read was meant to be written and published to impact the lives of anyone who comes across it. I hope you enjoyed it because there is plenty more story I have left to impact you with. Stay tuned for book #2!

www.ingramcontent.com/pod-product-compliance
Lightning Source LLC
LaVergne TN
LVHW021655060526
838200LV00050B/2357